# THE Revenge OF THE Ballybogs

SIOBHAN ROWDEN was born in Scotland and brought up in England. She has a degree in English and has worked as a holiday rep in Corfu, at Disney World in Florida and for a production company in London. The CURSE of the Bogle's Beard was her first novel. She lives in Brighton with her husband and children. She doesn't like beetroot or pickles.

www.siobhanrowden.com

# THE
# Revenge
## OF THE Ballybogs

## SIOBHAN ROWDEN

### Illustrated by Mark Beech

**SCHOLASTIC**

First published in 2013 by Scholastic Children's Books
An imprint of Scholastic Ltd
Euston House, 24 Eversholt Street, London, NW1 1DB, UK
Registered office: Westfield Road, Southam, Warwickshire, CV47 0RA
SCHOLASTIC and associated logos are trademarks and/or
registered trademarks of Scholastic Inc.

Text © Siobhan Rowden, 2013
Illustrations © Mark Beech, 2013

ISBN 978 1 407124 90 2

A CIP catalogue record for this book
is available from the British Library.

Printed by CPI Group (UK) Ltd, Croydon, CR0 4YY
Papers used by Scholastic Children's Books are made
from wood grown in sustainable forests.

1 3 5 7 9 10 8 6 4 2

This is a work of fiction. Names, characters, places, incidents
and dialogues are products of the author's imagination or are
use fictitiously. Any resemblance to actual people, living or dead,
events or locales is entirely coincidental.

www.scholastic.co.uk/zone

for the real LPI

# Prologue

Barnaby stumbled on a rock and fell face down in the foul boggy ground. Two large knobbly hands clamped around his shoulders, turned him over and hauled him to his feet. He looked up into the fierce black eyes of the most monstrous bogle he had ever seen.

The whole of the bogle's face was covered in prickly black hair. His long, crooked nose sprouted thick tufts of nostril whiskers, which waved menacingly in the air as he snorted in excitement. Barnaby's gaze travelled slowly down to the two big bottom teeth that poked out of the bogle's jutting jaw, almost reaching those terrible, fluttering nostrils.

Barnaby staggered forward, frantically looking around for a way to escape. But he was completely surrounded. More bogles appeared from every direction. They were closing in, burping and grunting in anticipation, herding him along the dark, muddy road towards the main square.

A small crowd had gathered there, looking up at a large wooden stage. A high timber frame stood in the centre, with two big slings dangling ominously down. Under the slings was a pair of enormous jars. Barnaby could smell the vinegar before he reached them and his knees began to tremble...

# CHAPTER 1
# Nightmares

Barnaby Figg sat bolt upright, gasping for breath, his pyjamas drenched in cold sweat. His little dog jumped on to the bed and looked at him quizzically, his head tilted to one side.

"It's OK, Morley," panted Barnaby, "just another nightmare."

Barnaby had had a lot of bad dreams lately. He pulled Morley close and sank his face into the soft fur. It felt warm and comforting.

"But those silly old bogles don't scare me," he whispered.

Morley licked Barnaby's face, then curled

up at the bottom of the enormous purple bed. Barnaby glanced over at the clock – 6.15 a.m. He sighed and slumped back on to his pickled onion embossed pillow and looked around his room. He and his parents had been living with his pickle-obsessed grandmother for about a year now, but he had only just got used to everything in her giant mansion being a disgusting shade of purple and shaped like a pickle.

A weak shaft of dawn light shone through the window. Barnaby got up, stretching his arms high and yawning loudly. He made his way over to the window and looked out. A huge neon sign lit up the morning mist, casting an eerie red glow around three colossal chimneys towering above his grandmother's immense factory.

Hogsflesh Pickle Company

Granny Hogsflesh – or *Ho-flay*, as she liked to pronounce it – was a pickling mogul, and employed nearly everyone in the whole town. None of her employees knew it, but she was half bogle. This meant that Barnaby was one-eighth bogle! It's never fun to find out that you are not completely human, and the very thought of Barnaby's ancestors sent a ripple of goosebumps up his legs and over his body. Bogles are spiteful, hairy creatures that live under the bogs in a smelly world beneath our own. One eighth may sound very little, but Barnaby knew that tiny fraction was inside him, silent and waiting. He didn't know what it was waiting for, but he *did* know that he didn't want to be spiteful or hairy.

Barnaby watched the red haze slowly evaporate around the huge factory, and banished all thoughts of bogles from his mind, concentrating instead on his day ahead. He was going to be very busy. It was the first day of the summer holidays, but he wasn't looking forward to the same sort of break that normal children were. Not many eleven-year-olds are the head of a department in a pickle factory. Granny had put him in charge of Special Pickles. Unlike the other children he knew, Barnaby enjoyed working during the summer holidays. He loved to pickle extraordinary things, like trees and flowers, creating whole pickled gardens. And with the Hogsflesh scientists, he got to experiment with plants, cosmetics and even rubbish, finding new ways to preserve everyday objects.

The only thing he disliked about his job was that he only worked with grown-ups. They were always very polite to him, but he sometimes missed people his own age. He often wondered what it was like to have a best friend or a brother or sister who he could play with, or even fight with. But he didn't have time to think about it for long; he was too busy.

Barnaby was brilliant at his job, and he had a packed day. At nine thirty this morning, the president of the National Conker Club was coming in to visit their pickled horse chestnut tree. Then he had a video call scheduled with a global skincare company, presenting the

Hogsflesh Pickles face cream – Pickollagen – "*preserving youthful skin*". And in the afternoon, he had to inspect the damage caused to the roof in the Special Pickle Hall at the factory. A huge explosion had sent one of the scientists flying through the ceiling when one of the experimental pickling programmes had gone horribly wrong.

The sound of his bedroom door creaking open interrupted his thoughts.

Barnaby turned as Morley's ears pricked up.

"Hello?" he called. But before he had time to do anything, Morley leapt off the bed and shot out of the door, yapping loudly.

"Morley!" hissed Barnaby. "Come back, you'll wake up the whole house. Everyone's still asleep."

Barnaby raced to the door just in time to see Morley tugging on something at the top of the large purple staircase. He was sure he heard a sharp squeal that didn't come from the dog. There was a loud ripping sound as Morley skidded backwards, his mouth stuffed with a scrap of clothing.

Barnaby raced along the corridor and just managed to grab his collar as a dark shape disappeared down the stairs. Morley strained against him, still barking, despwerate to charge down the steps.

"Morley, shh. What is it, boy?" Barnaby picked up the filthy scrap of clothing. A putrid stench drifted off it, reminding him of his nightmare and filling his body with a sickening dread.

"Bogles!" he whispered.

# CHAPTER 2
# Voices from the Cellar

Barnaby dropped the grubby piece of material. Morley immediately grabbed it and shot off down the stairs. Barnaby followed cautiously, making his way down two flights to the lower ground floor.

"Morley?" he called.

There was no sign of the dog. He continued along a wide corridor, eventually stopping at a narrow stone staircase which spiralled down to the cellar. Barnaby stood at the top and shivered. The cellar was where Granny used to practise the dark side of pickling: preserving revolting and sinister ingredients used in black magic. That was before her jealous bogle cousin, Belchetta Ballybog, had tried to get rid of Barnaby and his family with a poisonous pickled toenail and take over the Hogsflesh Pickle Company. But Granny had saved them, and Belchetta had fallen into a huge vat of dark pickling fluid, and there she remained, in the corner of the cellar, pickled in time.

Barnaby peered down into the gloom.

"Morley?"

He listened for the sound of scampering paws, but after hearing nothing, he turned to go. He wasn't allowed in the cellar. After the incident with Belchetta, Granny had decided to turn her back on the dark side. Barnaby's mum, Hatty Figg, was in charge of closing it down and informing all their clients who used the pickles to practise the dark arts. This was a very dangerous job, and she wouldn't let Barnaby anywhere near. This was fine by him. He started to make his way along the corridor but stopped abruptly. Voices were drifting up the stairs. Someone – or something – was in the cellar.

Barnaby turned and crept closer, straining his ears. He stood for a moment on the top step, the cold stone freezing his bare toes. It was very early and he was sure that Mum, Dad and Granny were still in bed. But he could definitely hear voices. Every part of his body wanted to run back to his room – except for the bogle part. Bogles are fearless, and that small fraction urged him down the dark spiral staircase. He cautiously descended towards a faint glow at the bottom, hesitating for a moment, as the memory of his nightmare crawled back into his mind again.

Barnaby gritted his teeth and carried on. He couldn't let the bogles scare him like this. And if they were in the house, then he was going to find them.

Finally he stood under a dull lamp in front of a huge oak door. He knew that the door wasn't actually wooden, but a special intruder-proof metal. The pickling that went on in the cellar was top secret. Unfortunately, he also knew that bogles could break into anything.

Barnaby's heart thumped loudly as he stretched his hand towards a key in the lock and gently pulled it out. Granny had shown him how to get into the cellar. He mustn't turn the key or alarm bells would go off.

He carefully pushed the key into a hole in the side of the lamp by the door, and a control panel dropped down. Barnaby typed in 666, Granny's lucky number. The door slid down into the floor, exposing a second door with an eye scanner attached to it. He pressed his eyes against the strange binocular contraption. It was totally black except for a red line which moved first from the top of the screen to the bottom, and then from left to right. A *ting* sound told Barnaby that the computer inside the special door recognized him.

He pressed his ear against the door. He could still hear muffled voices. He took a deep breath and pressed ENTER. As the door slowly slid up into the ceiling, a loud and windy belching noise drifted through the gap...

# CHAPTER 3

# Bogles in the House

The door opened fully, revealing a lumpy old lady, as wide as she was short. The folds of her baggy skin had a slight metallic sheen and her long, thin nose stuck out like a glinting machete. It was Granny Hogsflesh. Her shiny appearance was the side effect from a silver antidote she had taken after Belchetta Ballybog stabbed her with the poisonous pickled toenail. When she got annoyed, she glimmered menacingly, and now was no exception. Her hairy chins were wobbling like mercury.

"This is my life's work," she spat, spray flying

off her thick wet lips. "You can't expect me—"

She broke off when she realized the door had been opened, and belched loudly in surprise.

Barnaby stood in the doorway looking in. The cellar was a long, wide tunnel. Four cave-like rooms led off from either side. This was where the dark pickling took place, and it was full of gruesome ingredients – earwax, mucus, toenails, verrucas, assorted animal gases and worst of all, beetroot. Barnaby hated beetroot. Several large vats, all empty now, stood in a row down the centre. Barnaby's mum, Hatty Figg, stepped out from one of the rooms; her usually pretty face was twisted in frustration. A brown hair sprouted from her chin, and she hiccuped loudly – the only signs of her bogle ancestry.

"But, Mother—" she began, then stopped when she saw Barnaby standing by the door.

"What are you doing here?"

"I heard voices," he said. "I thought you were all still in bed."

"You are NOT allowed in here," she continued, her dark, curly hair springing around furiously.

"I know, but—"

She wasn't listening to Barnaby, but had turned angrily to Granny, who now seemed a lot calmer.

"You told me that you had removed his eye scan and he couldn't get in," she cried.

"Barnaby is Head of Special Pickles," answered Granny, coming towards him. "He must have access to all areas."

18

Barnaby backed off. Although he had grown fond of his granny, she still made him feel slightly queasy with her endless burping and saggy jowls. Besides, he couldn't bring himself to walk far into the cellar.

"Come in, Barnaby," said Granny, holding out a fleshy hand to him. "Look."

She pointed to a huge glass jar in a corner. "Belchetta Ballybog can't hurt you now."

It was very dimly lit, but Barnaby could just make out a figure floating in the liquid. He slowly walked in and stood before the jar. He stared up at Granny's pickled bogle cousin. Her sightless eyes seemed to glare back, the anger in them still perfectly preserved. Barnaby felt the blood draining from his head.

"Bogles," he muttered, as his knees gave way. "Bogles in the house…"

# CHAPTER 4
# The Railroad Ladder

Barnaby woke up to see three very worried faces peering into his own. Granny gave a loud belch and waved a small jar under his nose. The smell of rotting meat settled around him. He wasn't sure if it was coming from the jar or the burp, but he sat up straight, straining to get away from it.

"There we go," said Granny. "I told you dark pickles can also be used for good. The smell of pickled camel lips is great for reviving those who have had a nasty shock."

Barnaby looked around him, his head

throbbing. He was sitting in a big leather armchair in a perfectly round room with rows of books lining the high walls. A long ladder reached up from the floor to the ceiling. He was in the library. His dad, Fergus Figg, had joined them and was holding a damp flannel against a large bump on the side of Barnaby's head.

"Why does it have to be pickled camel lips?" asked Dad, taking the flannel off and examining Barnaby's lump. "Why can't you just give him a cup of sweet tea like an ordinary person?"

"Who wants to be ordinary when you can be extraordinary?" snapped Granny, elbowing him out of the way and gently replacing the flannel.

"Extraordinarily windy," muttered Dad.

"Shush, you two," said Mum, nudging them both out of the way and sitting on the arm of Barnaby's chair. "Are you feeling better, Barnaby?"

"I think so … what happened? Why were you and Granny arguing?"

"You fainted and banged your head on the floor. We had to get your dad to carry you up here," she said. "And we weren't arguing … much. Now, would you like to tell us what you were doing in the cellar?"

Barnaby sighed and put his hand up to feel the growing bump on his head.

"Morley chased something," he said. "Hey, where is Morley?"

"Morley's fine," said Dad. "He's waiting outside because he's not allowed in the library."

"He certainly is not," spluttered Granny indignantly, her rubbery lips spraying the surrounding area like a sprinkler. "I'll not have that dog slobbering all over my lovely books."

"I'm sure they're used to it," murmured Dad. "Anyway, what was Morley chasing?"

Barnaby looked round at everyone.

"I think it was … a bogle," he said.

Granny's eyes widened, Mum groaned and Dad slowly sank into another chair.

"Did you get a good look at it?" he asked.

"Well, I didn't exactly *see* it…" Barnaby broke off as everyone looked at him doubtfully. "But Morley had a smelly bit of cloth and … I thought he might have ripped it off a bogle… Bogle clothes are dirty and they stink … and it smelled like the bog … and…"

Mum put her hand over his.

"It could have been anything," she said, softly. "Morley is always carrying around smelly bits of rag."

"I know, but he seemed to tear it off something."

Dad got up and put his hands on Barnaby's shoulders.

"Did you have another nightmare last night?"

he asked, gently.

"Yes," said Barnaby.

"Bogles again?" asked Dad.

"I can't remember any more. It might have been bogles, or pickles, or pickled bogles – I don't know."

"I think it's time to move out of this place and back to our old house," said Dad.

Barnaby's parents really wanted to move back to their old home, a small wooden house on the edge of town, but each time they were about to go, Granny seemed to find a reason why they had to stay.

"It's the only thing that will stop these nightmares," continued Dad. "Barnaby needs to be in his own home."

"This is his home," snapped Granny, "and besides, you can't. The building work in your old house isn't finished yet."

Dad sighed.

"We didn't even want to make the place bigger," he said. "That was your idea. Are you sure you're not paying the builders to take as long as possible?"

Granny ignored him and tried to sit on the other arm of Barnaby's chair, but she was too short and her bottom was too big, so she gave up.

"The only bogle in this house is a pickled one," she said. "You saw her in the jar, and she's not going anywhere. The bogles will never trouble us again. You have nothing to worry about."

Barnaby sighed. Maybe it was just his imagination running wild after another nightmare.

"Why is Belchetta still here anyway?" he asked. "It's disgusting. You should have got rid of her ages ago."

"We know," said Mum. "But it's not that easy."

"Pickled bogle," whispered Granny, her bristly face glowing. "Some people would pay a fortune for that."

Barnaby's mum glared at Granny.

"For once and for all, Mother," she said, "we are not selling Belchetta's pickled remains."

Granny burped moodily and waddled over to the enormous ladder. It stretched from a track on the floor right up to a rail attached to the high ceiling.

"Is that why you were arguing?" asked Barnaby.

There was an awkward pause.

"I had better give the railroad ladder a quick whirl around," she said, ignoring the question and stepping on to the first rung of the ladder. "Just for maintenance purposes, you understand."

She pressed a button on a small remote control and started to travel around the circular room on the ladder. Barnaby's mum and dad rolled their eyes to the ceiling. The three of them sat in the middle of the room as Granny picked up speed and started flying round the library.

"She always does this," said Barnaby.

"I know," sighed his mum. "It's ridiculous at her age. Not to mention dangerous."

"I heard that," yelled Granny as she sped past them, her purple velvet dress flying out behind her.

"Anyway," said Dad. "I've got some news to tell you, and now is a good time while the old girl is getting her kicks."

"I heard that too!" she bellowed, but she didn't stop.

"As you know," continued Dad, "I wasn't completely happy about working at the pickle factory at first, but now, after a year, my pickled peas are doing extremely well."

"Can't see why," came the flying voice. "They're disgusting."

Barnaby couldn't understand how Granny could hear what they were saying, let alone comment on it. She was going so fast now, she was a blur. He hoped she had a strong grip. He tried to concentrate on what his dad was saying.

"Well, they are selling very well," yelled his dad, for Granny's benefit. "And I have been asked to be a guest speaker at the next LPI general meeting."

"What's the LPI?" asked Barnaby.

"The Ladies' Pickled Institute," said Dad, proudly. "Great supporters of the British pickle. Guardians of high standards and ethical practices. And I've invited the local branch here, for a factory tour."

There was a screech as the railroad ladder ground to a halt. Granny staggered off, her patchy silver hair hanging over one eye, her clothes rumpled and her face glowing angrily.

"Over my pickled body!" she thundered.

# CHAPTER 5
# Sprinkled Trotters

Granny and Dad argued all the way from the lilac library to the mauve breakfast room and all through their meal.

"You're just jealous that the LPI has never asked you to join them," said Dad, crunching his pickled cauliflower angrily.

"Rubbish," spat Granny, peppering the table with pieces of pickled pigs' trotters. "They've been trying to get me to join for years. They are after my recipes and now they're using you to get to me, you great nincompoop."

Barnaby watched as Granny's half-chewed

morsels sprinkled into his glass of milk and on to the pickled egg laid out in front of him for breakfast. Very slowly he slid it off his plate and under the table to a waiting Morley. It was only eight thirty, but it felt a lot later. All he had heard this morning was his family yelling at each other, and his head still ached from his fall.

"Spies, the lot of them," Granny continued. "And you've invited them into my factory."

"Can we please change the subject now?" said Mum, noticing Barnaby's pale face. She examined the bump on his head. "I think you need to cancel your meetings and take today off."

Barnaby just nodded slowly. He loved being in the factory and hated missing a day, but he did feel exhausted.

"You go back to bed," she said, giving his hair a ruffle. "I've got to get back to the cellar; I have a lot to get through today. That's why I was up so early."

"Me too," said Dad, glancing at Granny. "Some of us have top-selling recipes to perfect. Pickled peas are calling."

His mum and dad gave him a hug and left the room. Granny sat opposite Barnaby, buffing her silvery arms with a napkin.

"I tarnish very easily," she explained. "Do you want the day off, or would you like to come with me to the factory? I'll be showing off the Golden Gherkin that we won last week. But I also have to explain to the staff about that explosion in the Special Pickle Hall, and it might be a good idea if you're there. Everyone is talking about the scientist erupting through the roof."

"Have they found him yet?" he asked.

"No sign at all," said Granny. "It's a terrible

business – not good for company morale. I just don't understand how it could have happened. My health and safety record has always been impeccable."

"I know," sighed Barnaby, "Dr McLelland was a great scientist."

"So, are you coming then?" asked Granny.

Barnaby thought for a moment. He didn't feel up to meetings with global skincare companies and conker enthusiasts, but on the other hand he didn't fancy sitting in his room all day, thinking about pickled bogles.

"I'll come with you, Granny," he said at last.

She smiled and walked round the table to him. A low grumbling sound came from her enormous belly. Her face twisted as the rumble slowly made its way up through her chest, passing her quivering chins and eventually exploding from her sagging mouth. Barnaby sat in his grandmother's porky burp, not daring to breathe in until it had subsided.

"Good," she said. "Let's go."

They left the breakfast room and walked down the corridor to the great entrance hall, where Granny pinned on her tiny purple hat with a long feather sprouting from the top and pulled on her silky lilac gloves.

"One is ready to leave one's house now," she announced in her *I have my posh hat and gloves on* voice.

Morley sat by the huge front doors, whining. Barnaby gave him a reassuring pat as he reached for a long silver gherkin handle and hauled one open.

"You know you can't come to the factory with me, Morley," he said. "Don't cry, boy. I won't be long."

Granny squeezed through the doorway, but got stuck in the middle.

"You need to open both doors, you silly boy," she puffed, desperately trying to free herself.

*And you need to cut down on the pickled pigs' trotters*, thought Barnaby, as he struggled to hold both of the great doors open.

They eventually left the house and crossed the road to the huge factory. The curly iron gates stretched high above them. Entwined in the middle were the enormous steel initials HPC – Hogsflesh Pickle Company. The red-brick building towered behind the gates, its three main chimneys casting long shadows over the entire town in the early morning sun. A stooped security guard came out of the gatehouse. He was ancient, even older than Granny.

"Good morning, Mrs *Ho-flay*," he called.

"Good morning, Mr Brown," she said. "How are you this morning?"

"A bit stiff, ma'am, but…"

"I don't want to know any personal details, thank you," sniffed Granny. "Just let me into my factory, please."

The iron gates swung open and they walked through, Granny stomping ahead.

"Morning, Mr Brown," said Barnaby to the old man. "Sorry about that."

"Morning, Barnaby," he croaked. "Don't you worry, I'm used to her."

Barnaby followed Granny into the grand reception area. A white tiled floor stretched out before them, with a large mosaic of the company emblem in the centre: the purple initials HPC inside a white onion, which was inside a purple egg. Granny nodded to the receptionists, who stood to attention as she and Barnaby headed through a door and on to the factory floor. It was the size of an aircraft hangar. The walls and ceiling were white. Fluorescent lights lit up the huge hall, making it extremely bright. Rows of spotless white plastic tables covered the gleaming floor, with large signs at the end of each:

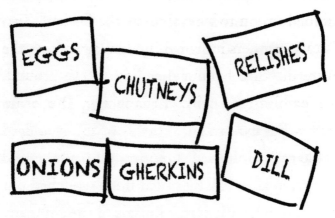

Many more stretched into the distance.

The factory workers stood behind their tables, dressed in mauve overalls with a dark company emblem on the back. Huge vats of vinegar lined the walls, but most impressive of all was a great glass office, suspended from the ceiling with a white corkscrew path circling its way from the centre of the hall all the way up to the top.

As Granny made her way past the rows of tables and staff, a hush filled the vast space. Barnaby waited at the bottom of the steps as she climbed up on to a podium at the far end. Two gigantic banners hung behind her, stretching the entire distance from the ceiling to the ground, one emblazoned with a giant egg, the other with a jumbo onion. This was the Standard Pickle Hall.

# CHAPTER 6
# The Scope-a-Phone

"Good morning, everyone."

Granny's voice blared out of several loudspeakers dotted around the hall.

"Good morning, Mrs *Ho-flay*," came the reply from hundreds of voices.

"Before I start, I would like to congratulate you all on our recent success at the British Academy of Fermenting and Pickling Arts annual awards ceremony."

The crowd began applauding.

"*Ho-flay* Pickles won not one, not two, but three BAFPA awards!"

A cheer went up, and the clapping got louder.

"*Best Supporting Condiment* went to our chutney department, for their revolutionary **Radish Relish.**"

More cheers.

"We retained our title for *Best Leading Pickle* with our **Perfect Piccalilli,**" she shouted above the noise.

"And finally, the top prize – The Golden Gherkin – awarded for *Outstanding Contribution to Pickling*, went to…"

Granny paused, her silvery cheeks flushed pink.

**"The Ho-flay Pickle Company!"** she yelled, holding up a large golden trophy in the shape of a huge gherkin.

The Standard Pickle Hall erupted in a massive cheer. People began to bang the tables and

41

stamp their feet in appreciation. The sound was deafening. Granny held the trophy high above her head, nodding her approval. When the cheering died down she began to speak again.

"The Golden Gherkin and the other BAFPAs will be on display in reception," she said. "They are here for all of you to see when you come into work each morning, a reminder of the pride and respect we have for our beloved company."

Granny wiped a tear from her eye before continuing.

"Now, on a more solemn note, you may have heard about the explosion that occurred next door in the Special Pickle Hall."

There was a loud murmuring as everyone

turned to discuss the incident with their neighbour.

"There are many rumours flying around," said Granny. "So I am here to tell you exactly what happened."

A hush descended again.

"Here in the Standard Pickle Hall we all work hard making pickles to be proud of, from our snack-sized pickled wrens' eggs to our "feed a family of four" ostrich eggs. Our colleagues next door in the Special Pickle Hall are also working hard. *Ho-flay* scientists are experimenting with pickles that will one day change the way we live, pickles that will improve civilization..."

As Granny's voice rose, the noise level began to grow again. People were nodding and clapping.

"Pickles of the future," shouted Granny. "Pickles that will enrich society, and advance the human race."

Barnaby looked round at the whooping workforce. He wondered what would happen if any of them found out that Granny wasn't actually a full member of the human race.

She waited for the shouting to die down, and then continued in a much quieter voice.

"Unfortunately, while the scientists were researching the possibilities of pickled plutonium, a mechanical failure led to an eruption of devastating force."

Hundreds of gasps and gulps bounced off the walls.

"Thanks to our pressurized vinegar reactor, no radiation leaks have occurred. However, one of our brave nuclear scientists, Dr McLelland, was blasted through the roof, never to be seen again."

There was a moment of silence as people bowed their heads in respect.

"When you are pushing boundaries," said Granny, solemnly, "when you are experimenting at the highest level, losses may occur. But never forget that it is better to have pickled and lost, than never to have pickled at all."

The cheering resumed, echoing around the hall, then died down as the first notes of the company anthem boomed from the loudspeakers. Hundreds of voices joined together to belt out "Long Live *Ho-flay* Pickle Company" as a huge flag bearing the company emblem was hoisted high above the crowd.

After three "Hip hip, *Ho-flays*", there was a final enthusiastic cheer; then a horn blasted and all the staff turned to their tables. Machinery whirred into action and vinegar vats began to bubble. Sharp knives glinted as hundreds of onions, eggs and cucumbers were sliced and diced to a loud chopping rhythm.

"I think that went well," said Granny, coming down from the podium. "But time to do some work now. Come on, we have to walk to my office this morning."

Barnaby looked up at the spiralling white path that led to the glass office dangling high above the hall.

"I'm afraid the Vinaigrette is parked at the top," she said.

The Vinaigrette was Granny's vinegar-powered three-wheeler car. Her pride and joy. She used it to get around the enormous factory. Barnaby felt relieved as they walked up the corkscrew path. The Vinaigrette was very nippy and Granny loved going dangerously fast.

They finally reached the top, where the round white car was parked outside the entrance to the glass office. Granny patted the bonnet as they stepped past into a small reception room. The glass walls were full of colourful chutneys and relishes, giving the room a red glow. Two ladies looked up from their computers as they came in.

"Good morning, Mrs *Ho-flay*," they said together.

"Good morning, Grace, morning … um … um … you," said Granny, walking past them towards the second, much larger room. "I need you to cancel all of Barnaby's meetings today."

Barnaby smiled at the ladies and followed Granny into her office. He always felt slightly dizzy as he looked through the glass floor at the purple workforce beneath. Suddenly the sound of Granny's booming voice filled the enormous hall.

## "I AM WATCHING YOU!"

Everybody glanced up at the glass office, and

then carried on chopping faster. Barnaby turned to see Granny looking down at the workers through a long telescope. A small microphone dropped down from the eyepiece and hung just in front of her mouth.

"MISS LEVESLEY," she blared.

Barnaby could just make out a small figure freeze beneath them.

"THE PRECISION OF YOUR CUCUMBER CUTTING IS OUTSTANDING. WELL DONE."

The figure appeared to relax and continued chopping.

"MISS RAVENSCROFT."

Granny's roving telescope had stopped on another poor member of staff.

"SLOPPY SLICING WILL DAMAGE THE QUALITY OF THE PICKLE AND THE REPUTATION OF THE *HO-FLAY* NAME. PLEASE CHOP NEXT TO MISS LEVESLEY AND FOLLOW HER LEAD."

Granny's telescope followed the tiny woman below as she shuffled across the factory floor. Granny turned the microphone off and looked up at Barnaby.

"What do you think of my new gadget?" she said. "It's a scope-a-phone."

"Well, it's, um…" he began. He wanted to say he thought it wasn't nice to spy on people, but he didn't want to make her cross.

"I knew you'd like it," she said. "As a captain of industry, I have a duty to keep my staff on their toes."

Standing there with her telescope, Barnaby thought she looked more like a captain of a pirate ship, but wisely kept the thought to himself.

Granny placed the scope-a-phone on her enormous glass desk and picked up the telephone. Behind her was her gruesome collection of pickled insects.

"Now, back to business," she said. "We really must sort out that hole in the Special Pickles roof."

"Granny?" said Barnaby, staring at the insects behind her. "Can I ask you a question about dark pickling?"

Granny's face lit up and she put the phone down. She pressed a button and all the glass turned a lurid shade of purple, making it impossible to see in.

"I knew you hadn't given up on the dark side, Barnaby," she whispered. "What do you want to know?"

# CHAPTER 7
# The Fly and the Bedbug

Barnaby didn't like the office glass turning purple. It made him feel trapped. He walked behind Granny's desk, still staring at her insect collection.

"I still think we should stop making dark pickles," he said, picking up a small jar and inspecting the fly inside. He heard her snort behind him. "I just wanted to know how you got into … you know … the dark side."

Granny stood up and took the jar from him.

"A housefly!" she said. "Horrible poo-eating creatures that spread disease."

He nodded.

"However," she continued, "in remote parts of the world, one housefly mixed with half a black pepper and one pinch of devil's dung spice can be applied to the eyes and is said to cure cold fever."

She picked up another jar. Barnaby peered in at the tiny but gruesome little insect.

"The common bedbug," said Granny. "It feeds on human blood at night and hides in cracks during the day – not nice." She handed the jar to Barnaby. "But, eaten in the right amounts, it can be an effective antidote for snake bites and can also promote hair growth."

Barnaby looked at her doubtfully.

"Look it up if you don't believe me," she said, pointing at the computer, "under 'medicinal insects'. What I'm trying to tell you is that nothing is completely good or completely bad, and it's the same with the dark pickles. Perhaps we should rename them 'grey pickles'."

Granny released another large belch and Barnaby quickly returned the bedbug to the shelf and moved to the other side of the office.

"Is that what you were arguing with Mum about?" he asked.

Granny nodded.

"Your mum wants to close down the whole of the dark pickles," she said. "I know that I agreed we would, after our horrible incident with Belchetta, but I have changed my mind. I think we should keep the pickles and just change who we sell them to. Make sure we know what they are being used for."

Barnaby thought for a moment.

"I bet you couldn't use a poisonous pickled toenail in a good way," he said.

"Well, that may be true," Granny said, "but that leads me back to your original question – how did I first become interested in the dark side?"

She glanced towards the door and continued in a barely audible voice.

"As you know," she whispered, "I had a human mother and a bogle father."

Barnaby nodded. He knew that many years ago, before Granny was born, her human mother, Mary Morley, had found a baby bogle on her family's beetroot farm. She had been cursed by the baby's mother, Burpina Ballybog, who thought she had stolen it. To break the curse, Mary had married Burpina's brother, Baldric Ballybog. A year later, Granny was born.

"I grew up in the bogle underworld, deep below the bogs in the Forest of Fen," Granny continued. "I was banished many years ago for turning my back on the bogles and living above ground with humans. But when I was a child, my cousin Belchetta and I would watch my Aunt Burpina grinding toe knuckles into powder to put into—"

"Grinding what?" asked Barnaby, in disbelief.

"Toe knuckles," repeated Granny, "same as finger knuckles, but on toes. My Aunt Burpina was an expert at making powerful bogle potions, and ground toe knuckles were an essential and potent ingredient."

Barnaby was beginning to wish he had never started this conversation.

"What sort of toe knuckles?" he asked.

"Anything that has toes will do," said Granny, "but mainly rats. Bogles are partial to a nice roasted rat for Sunday lunch."

Barnaby felt disgusted.

"That's horrible," he said.

"Not really," said Granny. "What does your mum do with the roast chicken bones?"

"Sometimes she boils them up and makes soup," he said.

"Well, bogles grind up their animal bones to make potions. It's not that different."

"I suppose…" muttered Barnaby.

"Toe knuckles are the key ingredient in a memory loss potion," Granny went on, "which, like everything else, can be put to good or bad use. Once, a distant bogle cousin of ours, Temper Tatty, became ill and his beard fell out. He was completely traumatized by the experience. There is nothing more shameful than a bald bogle. The more he worried, the more unwell he became, until it looked like he would never get better.

Aunt Burpina gave him some of her memory loss potion and he completely forgot about his baldness and eventually made a full recovery."

"I think I would rather go bald than drink toe-knuckle juice," said Barnaby.

"I agree," said Granny. "Given in large doses it can be lethal."

"What have toe knuckles got to do with the dark side of pickling?" asked Barnaby.

"I was inspired by the powerful ingredients my Aunt Burpina used in her bogle potions," whispered Granny. "So, many years later, when I began pickling eggs and onions, I also started pickling rare ingredients used in sorcery and witchcraft."

A sharp beeping sound interrupted their conversation. Granny turned pale and checked a small device in her bag. It looked like a phone, but there were fewer buttons and it was flashing red.

"It's the intruder alarm in the cellar!" she shouted, running for the door. "Hurry, your mother's down there."

Barnaby was already halfway out.

# CHAPTER 8
# The Underground Tunnel

They jumped into the Vinaigrette. Granny reversed at full speed down the curling white path to the factory floor, and for once Barnaby didn't care. People dived to safety as Granny tore through the Standard Pickle Hall towards a tunnel which led to the Special Pickle Hall.

"Where are you going?" cried Barnaby. "This isn't the way to the cellar. We've got to get back to the house."

"Trust me!" yelled Granny, hurtling towards the wall at the end of the great hall. Barnaby couldn't help closing his eyes as they seemingly sped through it. The tunnel connecting the two halls was hidden by an optical illusion. Granny screeched to a halt in the middle of the tunnel, pulled a lever in the Vinaigrette, and the road in front of them dropped down to form a slope. They drove down and jumped out at the bottom. The road immediately rose back up into the ceiling. Barnaby could just make out another smaller tunnel leading off to the left.

"Come on," shouted Granny. "This tunnel links the cellar to the factory."

Barnaby had heard about the underground tunnel before, but had never used it.

It was very dark and water dripped from the walls. He ran through, not caring, Granny puffing along behind him. They came to a door. Granny pressed her face against it and it slid sideways into the wall.

"It's a nose scanner," panted Granny.

"Everyone's nose is different."

They stepped into the far end of the cellar.

"Mum?" called Barnaby, looking frantically around. She wasn't by the earwax, mucus or verrucas.

"Granny, have you checked by the animal gases?"

He saw her staring into a corner. "What is it?" he asked.

"Empty," she muttered.

"I know it's empty," he said. "I can't find her anywhere."

"No, look," she whispered, pointing into the corner.

Barnaby hesitated. He knew it was the corner where Belchetta Ballybog's pickled remains were. He looked up into the huge glass jar. It was completely empty.

# CHAPTER 9
# The Feeble Chicken

A trickle of sweat ran down Barnaby's forehead. He tried to calm himself, but his breath came in quick spasms, making him feel dizzy. He was going to be sick. He staggered against a table. His granny's face floated in front of him. She held out her hands; she was going to catch him…

"Snap out of it!" yelled Granny, gripping his shoulders. "I'm trying to think, and you're staggering around like a feeble chicken."

Barnaby took a deep breath. "I'm sorry. I just panicked when I saw the empty jar."

"I am just as surprised as you," she said. "But

there is probably a very good reason. I think your mother has got rid of Belchetta after your little turn this morning. That's why she's not here. And she probably triggered the intruder alarm by mistake when she was leaving. It's easily done."

"OK," said Barnaby, knowing that it actually wasn't easily done. He was feeling uneasy but was trying his best to be brave.

"I'll stay here and wait for her to come back," said Granny. "You go to the factory and let your dad know what's happened. You can get back in through the tunnel. There's a lever in the Vinaigrette that will make the road drop down for you."

Barnaby hesitated. He didn't fancy going through the tunnel on his own, but he didn't like being compared to a feeble chicken either, so he set off to find his dad.

He dashed through the tunnel linking the cellar

to the factory. A large drop of water fell from the ceiling, landing on his cheek and making him jump. He could just make out the Vinaigrette still parked at the far end and sighed in relief, then stopped in his tracks. He saw a shadow in the car. It was very gloomy, but he was sure he saw some movement. Barnaby pressed his back against the damp tunnel wall, breathing deeply.

"I'm not afraid of bogles," he whispered to himself. "I've faced them before and I can face them again."

He edged closer along the tunnel, sidled up to the car and peered through the windscreen. It was completely empty. He told himself it must have been a trick of the light, and looked cautiously around before climbing in and locking the doors. He had to get out of there fast. He pulled down the white lever he had seen Granny use, and the ceiling in front of him dropped down, making a slope up to the factory tunnel. He had never driven a car before and was planning to get out and walk up the slope, but he couldn't bring himself to unlock the doors and step out.

Barnaby looked at the Vinaigrette's control panel. He knew it was keyless, and that Granny just pressed a switch to make the engine start up. He hadn't the faintest idea what any of the buttons and dials were for, but a bright red switch in the centre stood out from the rest. He reached out, hoping with all his might it was the ignition, and flicked it down. Immediately a torrent of pickled walnuts shot out from the exhaust pipe, ricocheting around the tunnel walls.

Barnaby yelled in surprise and quickly flicked the switch back up. The shower of walnuts stopped instantly. He studied the control panel again, breathing heavily. He remembered that Granny was in talks with MI6 about developing the Vinaigrette for use by their secret agents, and was terrified of what another button might do. A shiny green knob just above the steering wheel caught his eye. It had something written on it in tiny black letters. Barnaby leaned forward, straining his eyes to read it. The word GO had been scored out with a thick black line. *Strange*, he thought, rubbing his finger gently over the button. To his surprise the black line came off on his hand. He looked closer and was disgusted to find it was in fact a wiry black whisker. It didn't look or feel human.

"Ugh!" he shouted, flicking it on to the car floor. "Granny's chin is worse than I thought."

He wiped his finger on his trousers and rested it back on the button, took a deep breath in and pressed down. There was a cough and a chug as the engine started up.

"Phew!"

Next, he looked down at the foot controls. There was a brake pedal and an accelerator pedal, just like the dodgem car he had driven at the fair once. He bit his lip, shut his eyes and pressed his foot down on the accelerator.

The Vinaigrette shot up the slope like a rocket. Barnaby opened his eyes just in time to see the bricks of the factory tunnel right in front of him. He slammed on the brake and skidded right into the wall. There was a loud smash of plastic as he was thrown forward, but just as his head was about to hit the dashboard, an airbag in the shape of a huge pickled onion exploded open. Barnaby's face plunged into the soft material, but his relief turned to panic as the onion airbag continued to expand, filling the round car. It lifted him out of his seat, squashing him flat against the window. He groped around wildly, desperately trying to find the door handle as the airbag got bigger and bigger. His nose was flattened against the glass as it continued ballooning out of control. He tried to open his squashed mouth to scream for help as a huge POP filled the air, and a loud hissing told him that the giant airbag had burst. Very slowly it collapsed in a heap around him.

Barnaby sat there for a moment gasping for breath before staggering out to inspect the damage. The left side of the Vinaigrette was crumpled against the tunnel wall. It was ruined, and Granny was going to kill him.

# CHAPTER 10

## The Ladies' Pickled Institute

Barnaby reached inside the damaged car and pulled back the white lever, making the road behind him slot back into place. He couldn't understand how the Vinaigrette could have malfunctioned so badly, but he didn't have time to think. He had to find his dad as soon as possible.

He walked into the Standard Pickle Hall and looked around. He caught sight of his dad's red hair sticking up over a **Pickled Peas** sign and made his way over. Fergus Figg was surrounded by a group of extremely old ladies wearing visitor name badges.

"Oh, Mr Figg, I can't tell you how excited we are to be here," croaked the first one. She had jet-black hair and wore bright red lipstick. She smelled of lavender.

"The pleasure is all mine, Miss Jean," said Barnaby's dad, clearly enjoying all the attention.

"So what exactly goes into those delicious pickled peas of yours, Mr Figg?" asked another one.

"I would love to tell you – Miss Homely," said Dad, reading her name badge, "but I'm afraid that's classified information. I did write to your Lady Chairman, explaining that all our recipes are secret. Now, if you would like to follow me, I'll show you a *Ho-flay* pickled egg."

"No, I'm not going to beg," said Miss Homely.

"EGG," yelled a very tired-looking old lady beside her. "NOT BEG. She's a little hard of hearing," she explained.

71

"Thank you, Miss Boyle," said Dad. "I'll try to speak up."

Barnaby tried to nudge past the one called Miss Boyle and get his dad's attention. She turned and looked at him, or at least he thought

she looked at him. It was very hard to tell, as her eyelids sagged completely over her eyes like two small hammocks.

"Come to join the tour, have you?" she asked.

Barnaby looked behind, unsure if she was talking to him.

"Um … no," he said, "I'm just…"

"Good," whispered the old lady. "It's really boring. Get away while you can." She sighed deeply. "It looks like I'm going to miss my mid-morning nap."

"You've only just woken up from your early-morning nap," snapped Miss Jean. "Lovely Mr Figg has taken the time to show us around the factory and all you can think about is having forty winks."

"Who stinks?" asked Miss Homely, grabbing Miss Boyle and giving her a good sniff.

"WINKS," yelled Miss Boyle, pulling away indignantly.

Dad caught sight of Barnaby hemmed in and looking slightly worried.

"Ah, ladies, this is my son, Barnaby. Barnaby,

this is our local branch of the Ladies' Pickled Institute."

Barnaby smiled at them all as he squeezed past to join his dad.

"You're giving the LPI a tour?" he whispered. "Granny's going to be furious."

"I can handle the old goat," murmured Dad, ushering the elderly women along. "Now, this way to pickled eggs, ladies," he said.

"Dad, listen. I need to talk to you," muttered Barnaby as they walked across the factory floor. "In private."

He was engulfed in a waft of lavender as Mrs Jean elbowed past him and linked her arm through Barnaby's dad's.

"Why, Mr Figg, you have such lovely long legs," she said, red lips glinting. "I can hardly keep up."

Barnaby was joined by Miss Homely on one

side and Miss Boyle on the other. He glanced behind him to see two more old ladies. He was surrounded again.

"So how many of you are there?" he asked.

"Hair?" said Miss Homely, patting the steel bob that fitted her head like a helmet. "You like my hair? Thank you, dear."

Miss Boyle's baggy eyelids seemed to roll upwards.

"There are five of us here today," she yawned. "Mrs Ball, our Lady Chairman, couldn't make it."

"And the two behind?" asked Barnaby, warily.

"They've recently joined us from another branch," sniffed Miss Boyle. "The tall one rustles around like she's the queen of pickles, and the short one smells of meatballs."

They arrived at the pickled eggs department and Dad turned to the group.

"All our eggs come from free range—"

"Dad, can I have a word with you?" interrupted Barnaby.

"Not now, Barnaby," said Dad, frowning. "Can't you see I'm busy?"

He continued talking. Barnaby sighed and fell to the back of the group.

"Need to have a word with your dad, do you?" came a very deep voice from behind. He turned and the smell of meatballs hit him. It was the short old lady.

"Got something you want to tell him?"

Barnaby backed off slightly. Two sharp eyes glared at him from behind a mass of wiry grey hair. He felt like he was being inspected by an evil Brillo pad.

"Come and have a little chat with me instead," she said, grabbing his arm. She was very strong for someone so short. Barnaby tried to get his arm away, but couldn't.

"Meatballs," she growled.

"Excuse me?" said Barnaby

"They make you strong," she said. "I'm a great believer in meatballs."

Barnaby was beginning to feel a bit nervous.

"Oh … well, that's nice," he said.

There was a swishing noise beside them and the very tall old woman appeared. She was wearing a flowing green dress that rustled out behind her when she walked.

"Darling, you're scaring him," she breathed in a low voice. She held out a long wrinkled hand to him. "Barnaby, I'm Miss Rustling and this is my friend Mrs Wolfgruber. We are here to help you."

# CHAPTER 11
## Interrogation

Barnaby stared up at the tall old lady. Her long grey hair was flecked with red and piled high on top of her head, making her look even taller.

"Nice to meet you," he said. "But I don't need any help."

Miss Rustling and Mrs Wolfgruber exchanged an ominous look. They linked their arms through his and guided him further away from the rest of the group. He tried to shake them off, but Mrs Wolfgruber's thick fingers held him steady.

"You're missing out on the pickled eggs," he said, looking back over his shoulder. They led him to a quiet corner of the factory and forced him down on a chair.

"We have heard so much about you, darling boy," said Miss Rustling in her low breathy voice. "Apparently, you are a pickling genius."

"Thank you," said Barnaby, nervously. "But I haven't got time to talk now, so if you'll just excuse me…"

The two old women stood directly in front of him, blocking any means of escape.

"Word has spread in the pickling world of your achievements in preserving things other than food," continued Miss Rustling. "The LPI applauds innovative and forward-thinking picklers like yourself."

Barnaby wasn't listening. He was wasting time here.

"Is everything all right, Barnaby?" asked Miss Rustling.

"No, everything is not all right," he said, standing up. "I need to talk to my dad, and I've just been hijacked by two old—"

"Old?" boomed Mrs Wolfgruber, pushing him back down. "Who's old?"

"I just meant old-er," he said, frantically looking around for someone to save him. "Older – than me."

"You're scaring him again, dear," said Miss Rustling, laying a calming hand on Mrs Wolfgruber's arm. "Remember, we are here to … make friends with Barnaby."

She gave her friend a pointed look. Mrs Wolfgruber folded her arms and glared down at him.

"Now, where was I?" said Miss Rustling. "Ah yes, forward-thinking picklers. Beetroot and onions lie at the heart of what the LPI holds dear, of course, but Mrs Wolfgruber and I like to think of ourselves as a little … avant-garde."

Miss Rustling smiled and raised one eyebrow.

"Avant-what?" asked Barnaby.

"Garde, darling, avant-garde," cried Miss Rustling. "Not afraid to experiment."

Mrs Wolfgruber looked as confused as Barnaby.

"I didn't know I was avant-thingy," she said.

The smile on Miss Rustling's face faltered slightly.

"Of course you are, dear," she said through tight lips. "Look at how tirelessly you search for new ways to preserve your meatballs without turning them into mush."

"True," said Mrs Wolfgruber, nodding. "Haven't managed it yet, mind."

"You will eventually, my dear," said Miss Rustling, patting her friend's arm before turning to Barnaby. "And so, as fellow progressive picklers, we were wondering if you could show us around Special Pickles … and any other pickling places of interest that we don't know about."

"No," said Barnaby. "The Special Pickle Hall is out of bounds, and my granny wouldn't allow it."

Miss Rustling's face fell. She bent down awkwardly, to be eye-to-eye with him. He could hear Mrs Wolfgruber growling gently above him.

"Ah, the great Beatrix *Ho-flay*," said Miss Rustling. "Famous for her pickling prowess, yet has constantly refused to join the Ladies' Pickled Institute. I wonder why?"

She paused for a moment, looking intently into Barnaby's eyes.

"Your granny didn't want the LPI to have a tour at all, did she?"

"She likes to keep her recipes secret," said Barnaby, staring straight ahead and folding his arms. Granny had been right about the Ladies' Pickled Institute – they weren't to be trusted.

"Anything else we should know about Granny *Ho-flay*?" Miss Rustling went on. "Any other sort of … pickling that we don't know about?"

Barnaby looked quickly at Miss Rustling, then straight ahead again. Did she know about the secret in the cellar? He could feel his face going red.

"No, nothing," he said.

Miss Rustling sighed and stood up stiffly.

"Hmm," she muttered. "Maybe you would like to talk to Mrs Wolfgruber instead."

Barnaby edged to the back of his chair as Mrs Wolfgruber's face came close to his, and the whiff of meatballs settled around him.

"Like playing games, do you?" she barked.

"No," said Barnaby, thinking that spaghetti would never have the same appeal again.

"Then tell me about it."

"Tell you about what?" he asked.

"Tell me about…" Mrs Wolfgruber looked behind her and then from left to right. "… the dark side of pickling."

She was so close to him now that her deep voice seemed to vibrate his insides, turning them to mush.

"I – I don't know w-what you're talking about," he said, starting to feel queasy.

"TELL ME!" she thundered.

Barnaby felt like he was going to faint again, but then there was a swish of flowing clothes and Miss Rustling's long face appeared in front of him.

"You need to calm down, dear," she said to Mrs Wolfgruber. "Remember what the doctor said about getting overexcited. And look at the poor boy, he's turned quite pale."

Mrs Wolfgruber made a loud huffing sound and backed off.

"Now, Barnaby darling," whispered Miss Rustling, stroking a strand of his hair away from his face. "Like I said before, we are your friends, and friends share secrets."

Barnaby took a deep breath in. He felt glad that Mrs Wolfgruber had moved away. Then it suddenly occurred to him what the old women were up to. He had seen it on police TV programmes. They were playing their own version of good cop/bad cop – *good granny/bad granny*. Well, he wasn't going to tell them a thing. Mrs Wolfgruber was some distance away and he saw his chance. He pushed past Miss Rustling and made a run for it.

"You're not my friends," he called back over his shoulder, "and there is no secret."

He was close to the hidden tunnel which led

through to the Special Pickle Hall. He dashed in and pressed his back against the wall, waiting for them to pass, so he could go back in and search for his dad.

"Barnaby, come back," called Miss Rustling. "You're making a dreadful mistake."

Barnaby stood against the tunnel wall and watched the two old ladies shuffle past. He was just about to sneak back into the Standard Pickle Hall when a noise behind made him stop. He peered back into the gloom of the tunnel. He could just make out the wrecked Vinaigrette still crumpled against the wall, and a small figure climbing into it.

# CHAPTER 12
# Buff vs Grey

Barnaby felt torn. He still hadn't managed to tell his dad that Belchetta had gone missing and that his mum was nowhere to be found. But he had to find out who was in Granny's crashed Vinaigrette. If they found the lever which made the road drop away to the tunnel below, then they would find the cellar, and Granny's dark pickling secret. Slowly he edged his way along the tunnel wall. He could see the figure moving around in the car.

As he approached the Vinaigrette, he took a deep breath and called out.

"Hey! Stop right there."

The figure in the car froze. Then the door slowly opened and a bent and wrinkled creature clambered out.

"Is this the ladies' room, dear?"

"Miss Homely!" cried Barnaby. "What are *you* doing in the car?"

"No, I'm not looking for the bar," she said, "I'm looking for the ladies' room."

"Not 'bar' – CAR," he said loudly. "What are you doing in the CAR?"

"Oh, car," she said, looking slightly confused. "Is that what it is? I thought it was one of those modern lavatory cubicles."

"No, you're in completely the wrong place," said Barnaby, taking her gently by the arm. "Come with me."

"What a nice young man you are," said Miss Homely. "Willoughby, isn't it?"

"No, it's Barnaby."

"I thought so. Thank you so much, Willoughby."

"No, it's . . . never mind. Come on, Miss Homely. Let's go and find the others."

They found Dad and the rest of the LPI back by the pickled peas. Miss Rustling and Mrs Wolfgruber had rejoined the group and nudged each other when they saw Barnaby arriving with Miss Homely on his arm.

"Ah, Barnaby, Miss Homely, there you are," said Dad. "I was beginning to wonder if everyone had got bored and gone home."

"Is it time to go home?" asked Miss Boyle, who had fallen asleep in a nearby chair. Miss Rustling tutted and went to stand next to Barnaby's dad.

"How could we possibly get bored, Mr Figg,"

she said, "listening to a man so passionate about his peas?"

"Thank you, Miss Rustling," said Dad, smiling. "I see that we have more in common than just red hair."

Miss Rustling's cheeks went pink and she patted her high hair.

"How kind of you to notice," she said. "But I'm afraid it's no longer red, more 'buff' now."

"Buff?" said Miss Boyle, creaking to her feet. "Don't you mean 'grey'?"

Miss Rustling looked down her long nose at Miss Boyle's peppery locks.

"*You* have grey hair, dear," she said, icily. "Redheads don't turn grey, they turn buff."

"Looks grey to me," said Miss Boyle, folding her arms.

Mrs Wolfgruber pushed past everyone and stood directly in front of Miss Boyle, her hands on her hips.

"If Miss Rustling says her hair is buff," she boomed, "then it's buff."

It looked like there was going to be a big argument. Barnaby took the opportunity to get his dad's attention.

"Dad, I really need to talk to you," he said.

"Hang on a minute, Barnaby," said his dad. "This looks like it's going to be fun."

Miss Jean had squeezed herself in between Miss Boyle and Mrs Wolfgruber.

"Ladies, ladies, please control yourselves. Miss Rustling has lovely hair," she said, smiling up at her. "But it's definitely grey."

"Dad, please," said Barnaby, pulling him away from the little group. "We can't find Mum."

"What?" said Dad. He was finding it hard to hear above the shouts of "BUFF" and "GREY" coming from behind him.

"Granny said not to worry," continued Barnaby, "but Belchetta Ballybog has gone missing, and we don't know where Mum is."

The colour drained from Dad's face as Miss Homely wandered by.

"Apparently, there's a bar round here," she muttered.

Dad waited till she passed.

"Why didn't you tell me this before?" he said.

"I tried," whispered Barnaby, "but you wouldn't listen."

Dad made his way back to the still-arguing LPI.

"I will be informing our Lady Chairman, Mrs Ball, all about your behaviour," shouted Miss Jean.

"Who cares about Mrs Ball?" yelled Mrs Wolfgruber. "*I* shall be informing our National President, Miss Can-Can."

There was a sharp intake of breath from all the old ladies.

"Excuse me, ladies," said Dad.

They all completely ignored him.

"Impossible!" screeched Miss Boyle. "Everyone knows that Miss Can-Can is in New Zealand, researching ancient Maori pickles."

Mrs Wolfgruber was about to reply when Miss Rustling laid a calming hand around her shoulder.

"Now, now, darling, we don't want to say too much, do we? And besides, Mr Figg is trying to tell us something."

"I'm afraid that I am going to have to cut our tour short," said Dad, hurriedly. "Barnaby and I have urgent business to attend to. Thank you all for coming. Now, I'll just fetch someone to see you out."

As Dad grabbed a passing member of staff and

asked him to escort the LPI to the factory gates, Miss Rustling slipped a small green card into Barnaby's hand.

"If you change your mind, and have anything you want to tell us," she whispered, "anything at all – call me."

Barnaby looked at the card, which had Miss Rustling's name and telephone number printed in curly gold letters. Then as soon as she turned around, he flicked it into a nearby bin.

# CHAPTER 13
# The Pickled Lock of Hair

"Come on," said Barnaby, leading his dad through the factory floor to the hidden tunnel. Just as they were approaching, Granny Hogsflesh emerged. The wiry hairs of her eyebrows were knotted together in a terrible frown, and her silvery sheen had turned a dull grey.

"She's found the Vinaigrette," murmured Barnaby. "I am in so much trouble."

"What are you talking about?" asked his dad. But Granny had already reached them. Her cheeks were red and she was panting.

"Granny, I'm really sorry about the

Vinaigrette," said Barnaby. "It was an accident. I was just..."

"We haven't got time to worry about that," she interrupted. "Thank goodness I found you so quickly. Something terrible has happened."

"What is it?" cried Dad. "Where's Hatty?"

Two nearby workers looked up from their chopping stations.

Granny glared at them.

"Got something more interesting to do than pickle?" she barked.

They quickly resumed their slicing.

"It isn't safe to talk here," she said in a low voice. "Back to the cellar, as quickly as possible."

Granny led them past the wreckage of the Vinaigrette. Barnaby expected her to open it and pull the lever which made the road drop down, but instead she took a small device out of her handbag. It was the same one that had alerted her to intruders in the cellar. She pressed a button on it and a round circle in the floor the size of a manhole flipped open like a submarine hatch.

"We're going to have to use the Emergency Access Chute," she said, glaring at Barnaby. He glanced guiltily at the Vinaigrette.

"Follow me, and be quick about it," yelled Granny, jumping into the black hole in the floor. She was gone in an instant. Dad peered down it, sighing deeply.

"Why can't she just have stairs?" he asked, leaping in and disappearing into the darkness. Barnaby sat on the edge of the hole, his legs dangling down. He closed his eyes and pushed off, landing on a smooth plastic surface which sloped sharply down and around. He whizzed along in the dark, turning in a complete circle before shooting out of a hole in the tunnel wall where Dad and Granny were standing waiting for him.

"Come on," said Granny, pulling him to his feet and leading them through the dripping tunnel to the cellar. "I have informed the engineering team in Special Pickles to take the Vinaigrette to maintenance, but we have a far bigger problem on our hands right now."

Her voice was shaking, which worried Barnaby enormously. He was used to Granny sounding surly, but never scared. She pushed her face into the door, which scanned her nose and slid to one side, revealing the cellar behind.

"Quickly," she said, ushering them in.

The door clunked into place behind them.

"Right," demanded Dad. "Could you please tell me exactly what is going on? Where is Hatty?"

Granny handed him a note. As Dad read it, his knees seemed to sag.

"Kidnapped!" he whispered.

Barnaby felt a familiar sick feeling creeping through his body. His dad had disappeared last year – held prisoner by Belchetta down in the depths of Bogle Bog – and now it looked like it was his mum's turn to vanish.

"What?" he cried. "Let me see."

He snatched the note from his dad's hands.

The scrawled letters were written in black ink which had dripped down the green page, making it hard to read.

Beatrix Hogsflesh,
You may be interested to know that we have taken your daughter. All that we require for her safe return is the Hogsflesh Pickle Company. I'm sure you will agree, this is a small price to pay.

We will be in touch soon to arrange the transfer of all Hogsflesh Factory deeds. If you pay, we will send your daughter back. If you don't pay, then we will still send her back.

PICKLED!

Yours sincerely,

BB

P.S. Please find enclosed a small token of our intentions.

Barnaby looked at Granny, who held up a small glass bottle.

"It's a lock of your mother's hair – pickled," she said. "I found it with the note."

Dad snatched it out of her hand.

"Where did you find it?" he asked, urgently.

"It was on the table in the beetroot section," said Granny. "I was waiting for Hatty to come back. I was sure she had gone to get rid of Belchetta, because of what happened this morning with Barnaby. Then I noticed that some of the pickling equipment had also gone missing – three large vats and some malt vinegar. I started to check if any of the dark pickles had been taken, and found the ransom note on the table in the beetroot cave. I came up to find you immediately."

Dad took the note from Barnaby.

"BB," he said, reading it through again. "Any ideas?"

"Isn't it obvious, you great fool?" shouted Granny.

Dad spun around.

"Don't you call me a fool," he yelled. "If it wasn't for you and your stupid dark pickles, Hatty wouldn't be in this mess. It was you who put her in charge of closing down the dark side.

If you—"

"What do you mean, 'isn't it obvious'?" interrupted Barnaby.

"It's Belchetta Ballybog," cried Granny. "I think she's been resurrected … brought back from the dead."

There was a horrible silence. Barnaby tried to swallow but his mouth was too dry.

"Is that possible?" he croaked.

"Anything is possible with black magic," whispered Granny. "Especially bogle black magic."

# CHAPTER 14
# The Black List

"Of course it's not possible," said Dad, placing a reassuring hand on Barnaby's shoulder. "You can't raise people from the dead. Why do you say these things, Beatrix? Can't you see you're scaring the boy?"

"Well, maybe he should be scared," snapped Granny. "I heard stories about it, when I was a child."

"And that is all they were – *stories*," said Dad. "There must be other BBs. Belchetta is not back again. We all saw her this morning, and she was well and truly pickled."

Dad paced the cellar, reading the note over and over again.

"What about the LPI?" said Barnaby. "They were a strange bunch of old ladies."

"The LPI?" repeated Granny, marching up to Dad. "I said they were not allowed to step foot in my factory."

"I had already invited them," said Dad, still pacing. "I couldn't very well turn them away."

"Of course you could, YOU TWIT," shouted Granny.

"DON'T YOU CALL ME A TWIT," Dad yelled back.

"Will you two stop arguing," cried Barnaby. His head was spinning. "We all need to calm down and think."

Granny folded her arms and sat down, still glaring at Dad, who continued his pacing.

"Did any of the LPI have the initial B?"

Barnaby asked.

"Well, there was Mrs Wolfgruber, Miss Rustling, Miss Jean, Miss Homely and—"

"Miss Boyle," said Barnaby, "but I don't know her first name."

"Betty," said Granny, sourly. "Betty Boyle."

"But she didn't leave my sight," said Dad. "She was with me all morning."

"I've known of her for years," said Granny. "She's been trying to get her hands on my recipes for a long time. She's a pickle-stealing old trout, but I very much doubt she's a kidnapper."

"And I doubt she could stay awake long enough," said Barnaby. "Are there any other ideas?"

"We don't need any other ideas," wailed Granny. "I'm telling you it's Belchetta Ballybog."

"Nonsense!" cried Dad. "Stop saying that. It could be a disgruntled factory worker."

"Impossible," said Granny indignantly. "All my staff adore me."

Dad coughed loudly. It sounded very much like the word "rubbish".

"Then it must be one of your shady clients," he said, "angry with you for closing down the dark side."

Granny frowned and disappeared inside one of the cave rooms, muttering quietly. Barnaby could hear her keys jangling, followed by the rustling of paper. She eventually emerged holding a black file.

"This is the Black List. All the contact details of my dark clients," she said, placing it on the table. "Your mother had to contact these people to inform them that we were no longer supplying dark pickles. But I'm telling you it's a waste of time."

Barnaby and his dad crowded round Granny

to get a better look at the list of names.

"Let's have a look under B," said Dad.

## B

*Miss S Banshee (Ailech, Ireland)*

*Mr E Blackbeard (Bahamas, Caribbean Sea)*

*Mr E Blofeld (Warsaw, Poland)*

*Miss T Bloodlover (Transylvania, Romania)*

*Mr X Bonebreaker (New York, USA)*

*Mr A Bogeyman (No fixed abode)*

*Miss L Borgia (Rome, Italy)*

*Mr T Burton (London, England)*

"There!" said Granny, closing the file. "I told you it was a waste of time. None of my clients have the initials BB."

"We can't rule them out, though," said Dad.

"What about other bogles?" asked Barnaby, cautiously.

Dad stopped pacing and looked at Granny.

"It can't be," she said, shaking her head. "What would other bogles want with my factory?"

"Same thing as Belchetta," said Barnaby.

"She only wanted it because *I* had it," said Granny. "She wanted everything I had."

"But there could have been others who were jealous of your success," said Barnaby. "Can you remember any more names from your childhood?"

Granny thought for a long time.

"I can't," she said at last. "I've blocked most of my bogle memories out. I can only think of Belchetta, of course, and my father, Baldric Ballybog, but he died a long time ago."

They were all quiet for a moment, thinking of what to do next.

"Shouldn't we call the police?" asked Barnaby.

Granny looked warily around the cellar.

"There are going to be a lot of awkward questions," she said, glancing up at the pickled verrucas sign.

"Barnaby's right," said Dad. "We can't risk Hatty's safety just because of your twisted pickling."

"Maybe," said Granny, "but I don't think the kidnappers would be very happy if we got the police involved. It would probably make matters worse. We are going to have to play this one very carefully. Let me have a look at that ransom note again."

Granny took the letter from Dad. She studied the muddy green paper closely, and then slowly raised it to her nose and sniffed.

"Oh no," she whispered. "I knew it, I knew it! Bog paper … it's written on bog paper."

# CHAPTER 15
## Bog Paper

"What on earth is bog paper?" asked Dad, continuing his pacing marathon.

"Bog paper is made from the roots of swamp oak. It's used in all bogle correspondence," wailed Granny. She too began to pace up and down. "I told you she was back. Belchetta Ballybog is back from the dead and has taken my daughter."

Barnaby watched as the two of them flapped around the cellar like two flightless birds – a tall thin ostrich and a short fat turkey.

"Impossible!" cried Dad. "People do not come back from the dead."

"Belchetta is not a person," screeched Granny. "She is a BOGLE!"

Dad was about to reply, but Barnaby held his hands up and stood between them, stopping them in their tracks. He suddenly felt oddly calm inside, despite the circumstances.

"We have to think of a plan," he said, turning to Granny.

"The boy's right," she said. "It's time to take action."

They all sat down at the table.

"We must return to Bogle Bog," said Dad, grimly. "I know how to get there. I'll never forget being held prisoner in Belchetta's house by her and her cronies."

"What cronies?" asked Barnaby. "I thought it was just Belchetta."

"There were at least two other bogles there," said Dad. "They were very old and doddery and

I hardly saw them, but I could hear them all talking. I can remember how to get there, so I think I'm in the best position to go."

"You can't go," said Granny. "You'll stand out a mile. Bogles are half your height. If Hatty is being held there, the bogles will move her, and then we will never find her."

"I'll go," said Barnaby. The thought made him feel sick, but he had to rescue his mum. "I could disguise myself as a bogle."

"No," said Dad. "It's too dangerous."

"I will go," said Granny. "I know the bogles. I know how they work, and I know Bogle Bog."

"But you told me you were banished," said Barnaby, "and could never return."

"There's always a way round these things," she said, thoughtfully.

"Then let me come with you," pleaded

Barnaby. "I know Bogle Bog too. I'm one-eighth bogle!"

Dad got up and resumed his pacing.

"It's too dangerous," he repeated.

Barnaby stood up and caught hold of his dad's arm, making him stop.

"I went to the bog when I rescued you," he said, "and I can do it again. Please, Dad."

Dad sighed and put his arm around him.

"I'm proud of your courage," he said, "but—"

"Let the boy go," interrupted Granny. "Let him show that courage. I won't let anything happen to him. I'm going to bring along a selection of pickles to help us."

Dad still looked uncertain. "I'm coming too," he said.

"But you're too tall," said Granny. "You could jeopardize everything. Besides, we need you here in case Hatty escapes and manages to return.

And someone has to look after the factory while we're gone."

There was a long pause as Dad thought it over.

"OK," he sighed. "But if you haven't returned in twenty-four hours, then I'm coming after you."

Barnaby's stomach did a flip. He was going back to Bogle Bog.

# CHAPTER 16
# The Mucus Cave

"Right, that's settled then," cried Granny, jumping up from the table. "There's no time to lose."

Granny grabbed a bag and disappeared into one of two caves marked **Animal Gases**, while Dad opened the security door leading into the house.

"I'll get you some supplies from the kitchen," he said, "to eat on the way."

Barnaby's stomach was still churning and he didn't know if he could eat any lunch. The smell of flatulent fauna wafted from the cave Granny was in, making him feel even worse. He stood at the mouth and peered into the gloom. Granny was on a small stepladder, putting some bottles into her bag.

"What pickles are you taking?" he asked.

"The selection isn't great," said Granny, peering at each bottle in turn. "Your mother got rid of a lot of stock while closing down the dark side. But I've managed to salvage a turkey trump and some worm burps."

"How will they help us?"

Granny emerged from the Animal Gases cave.

"Turkey trumps are powerful things," she said. "The slightest whiff can knock a fully grown man to his knees, while the gas of a worm burp can affect the central nervous system, causing involuntary muscle spasms. It doesn't last very long, but if we find ourselves in a tricky situation, they could come in handy."

Granny looked around the cellar.

"We're all out of verrucas and earwax," she sighed, "and I'm not going near the toenails after my last experience. Go and see what's left in the mucus cave, Barnaby, while I get some beetroot."

"What are you going to use the beetroot for?" he asked, making his way over to the mucus cave.

"I don't know yet," she called, "but one thing we *do* know is that it's very powerful stuff. Never underestimate the power of a beetroot."

Barnaby didn't particularly want to enter the mucus cave and had to keep reminding himself that it was for his mum. He stepped inside. It was colder and darker than the rest of the cellar. He could just make out a lamp dangling from the damp ceiling and looked around for a light switch. It was just beside him, but was covered in a green slime that dripped from the walls and ceiling. He closed his eyes and stretched out his finger towards the switch, felt it sink into the cold goo as the lamp clicked on. He opened his eyes, but the lamp hardly gave out any light at all. He could just make out rows of empty shelves.

"All that for nothing," he muttered, turning to go. But as he was about to reach for the slimy light switch again, a flash of green in the far corner caught his eye. It was a large jar sitting on its own right at the back. Barnaby edged deeper into the cave. It was very slippery and he didn't want to end up on the sludgy floor. He picked up the heavy container and tried to read the label. But it was covered in large globules of slime. It appeared to be full of a yellowy-green jelly.

Granny's voice bellowed from outside the cave.

"Is there anything left in there?" she called.

Barnaby emerged holding the slimy jar. Granny's face lit up.

"Excellent," she beamed. "Rhino sneeze."

"There was only one left," he said. "What can we use this—"

But before he could finish, the heavy jar slid out of his slippery hands and fell towards the hard stone floor.

Quick as lightning, Granny dived to the ground, catching it before it smashed to smithereens.

"Silly boy," she cried from the ground. Her hair had fallen across one eye and her dress had crumpled up her tree trunk legs. "It's a good job for you I am in the under 70s ladies' rugby team."

Barnaby stared at his grandmother in astonishment.

"I'm really sorry, Granny," he said, helping her to her feet.

"I should think you are," she grumbled, placing the rhino sneeze on to the table and straightening out her purple dress. "The rhino had a particularly nasty cold at the time of this sneeze. Look at the quality of that mucus."

She gently shook the jar and watched its contents wobble like lime frog spawn.

"The cold virus is still encased inside," she said, carefully putting it into her large bag. "Whoever comes into contact with this pickled sneeze will instantly catch a stinking cold."

At that moment, Dad came back into the cellar through the double security doors. His red hair had drooped over his worried face.

"Right," he said, handing Barnaby a small rucksack. "I've packed you some food and drink for the journey."

He crouched down and looked searchingly into Barnaby's eyes.

"I can still come with you," he said. "It's not too late."

"I'll be fine, Dad. I've got Granny, and we'll take Morley with us for extra protection."

Dad stood up and looked at Granny. Barnaby was expecting them to start yelling at each other like they usually did. But Dad was silent as Granny placed a hand on Barnaby's shoulder.

"I won't let anything happen to my grandson," she said.

Dad nodded slowly and gave Barnaby a big hug.

"Keep your wits about you," he said, "and remember – never trust a bogle."

Barnaby hugged his dad back. He had a knot in his stomach and a lump in his throat.

"Come on, Barnaby," said Granny. "It's time to get your mother."

# CHAPTER 17
# Into the Forest of Fen

Barnaby and Granny fetched Morley from the big purple mansion and then headed out of town towards the great Forest of Fen. They passed several people who nodded respectfully to Granny.

"Act as if nothing has happened," she whispered to Barnaby. "We don't want to start a panic."

They both smiled and nodded back.

"They'll wonder where we're going," whispered Barnaby, through a big fake smile, "and why we're not at the factory."

"We are just taking the dog for a walk," she said in a loud voice. "Come on, Morley."

The little dog scampered between Barnaby's legs, glad to be out and about. Granny's dark pickles clinked loudly together in the big bag she was carrying, as they left the town behind and approached the edge of the forest.

Barnaby's breath quickened as they stepped beneath the dense canopy and on to a small track that led to the marshes which dominated the forest. Bogle Bog lay deep beneath them and the only way to get to it was by sinking down into a stinking swamp. The woods were horribly still and silent. Not a bird was singing or an insect humming. The only sound was Granny chewing on a pickled beef tongue a little way ahead of him, and Morley rooting around the bushes. He felt he had to break the silence.

"Earlier on, in the cellar," he began, "you said that you could never…"

He stopped mid-sentence at the sound of a large stick snapping behind them, and spun around. Morley's ears pricked up and he stood completely still, sensing something or someone close by.

"I said what?" said Granny, now gnawing on a piece of gherkin.

Barnaby signalled for Granny to be quiet as he scanned the forest behind them. There was nothing, not even the swish of a leaf.

"What is it?" she whispered.

"I thought I heard something."

They were still for a moment, listening to the silence that wrapped around the trees. Then a low rumble began to shake the surrounding leaves. It grew louder until the very ground beneath them started vibrating. Morley began barking. Barnaby's hair was swept up with the force and suddenly he was engulfed in a cloud of pickled beef tongue and gherkin. He turned just in time to see Granny's jowls settle after the intensity of a huge burp.

"Cow tongues," she explained, "delicious, but not good for the internal gases."

"Well, don't eat any then," coughed Barnaby, staggering away.

"Do you want some?" she said, offering a jar to him. "You haven't had anything to eat yet."

Barnaby glanced down at the long slab of pink muscle and felt his stomach contract.

"Still not hungry," he managed to say.

Slowly, they made their way through the forest. Every so often Morley would stop and look behind them, a low growl escaping from his soft muzzle. Barnaby hoped it was rabbits that Morley could see, but he had a horrible feeling that they were being watched.

Granny seemed totally oblivious to any noises, and carried on stomping through the overgrown path.

"Earlier on," said Barnaby, remembering what he was going to say before he was interrupted by Granny's huge burp, "you said that you could never return to Bogle Bog, because you were banished years ago for turning your back on the bogle community."

"That's right," she said. "My Aunt Burpina banished me after my parents died."

"Why? What happened?"

"Well, I was eighteen years old and still living in Bogle Bog when my mother and father caught a terrible disease called Marsh Fever."

"What's that?"

Granny's already furrowed brow pushed together even more, making it hard to see her eyes.

"First your temperature shoots up to over forty degrees," she said. "You start to shiver and sweat uncontrollably, and you forget who you

137

are. Then your skin turns the colour of the bog, a dreadful sludgy green, your eyes turn yellow and glaze over, your tongue swells up, and if it's really bad, you can die."

"That sounds horrible," said Barnaby.

"After my mother died," said Granny, sadly, "I went to tell my human grandparents above ground. By the time I returned, my aunt told me that my father had gone too. I was so upset that I went straight back to my grandparents' farm and never returned to Bogle Bog."

"Never?" asked Barnaby.

"No," said Granny. "Not even for their funerals. I couldn't face it."

They stopped for a moment and sat down on a tree stump to have a drink.

"About six months later," Granny continued, "I was visited by my Aunt Burpina. She asked if I was ever going to return to the bog. By that time, I had met your Grandpa *Ho-flay*, and I didn't want anything more to do with the bogles. I wanted to live above ground in the human world, and pickle my way to a fortune. I told her I was ashamed of my bogle heritage and so she banished me for ever. She said if I were ever to jump into the bog which led down to the village, then I would just sink and drown."

"Did you care?" asked Barnaby.

"Not one bit," said Granny. "Without my parents there, I never wanted to go back to the bog again, and never thought I would have to. My Aunt Burpina never liked me, and she despised my mother. She hated all humans."

"I thought every bogle hated humans," said Barnaby.

"Not hate, exactly," she replied. "They mistrust them, and they love to annoy them – creeping into houses and making a mess, that sort of thing."

Barnaby shook his head. He hated being related to these strange creatures.

"So how are we going to get into Bogle Bog, then?" he asked.

"Let's think about it over some lunch," she said, rummaging through his rucksack. "We've got some pickled onions and eggs, pickled gherkins and some beef tongue."

"Any apples?" asked Barnaby, hopefully.

"Yes," said Granny, disapprovingly. "But just have one. Too much fresh produce isn't good for you. We'll have to eat while we walk. I don't want to waste any more time."

They trudged on in silence, Barnaby crunching his apple, Granny sucking her eggs. "It looks like I'm going to have to sink down into Bogle Bog on my own," he said at last. He felt terrified as he uttered the words, but was desperately trying to sound brave. "You can wait for me by the swamp."

Granny shook her head, unable to speak, as she had just shoved a whole egg into her mouth. Bits of errant yolk were swept up by her thick tongue as they popped out on to her wet lips. Barnaby couldn't watch and looked up into the trees, waiting for her to finish.

"You can't go on your own," she said. "It's too dangerous. I'm going to have to risk it and come with you. Burpina Ballybog passed away many years ago. Her banishment will have died with her and I won't sink and drown."

"No," said Barnaby, firmly. He didn't want to take that chance. Granny Hogsflesh might not have the best table manners or social skills in the world, but he certainly didn't want her to drown in the bog.

"Well, what *are* we going to do, then?" she said. "We've got to get to your mother as fast as—"

They both jumped at the sound of another twig breaking. Out of the corner of his eye, Barnaby saw a dark shape flitting behind a nearby tree.

He edged towards Morley, who was growling quietly.

"Easy, boy," he whispered, reaching for his collar.

But Morley dashed towards the tree, barking wildly. A small figure ran out and disappeared into the undergrowth. Morley tore after it and also vanished from sight.

"I'm going after them," yelled Barnaby.

"Wait for me," shouted Granny, but he was already pounding his way through the thick vegetation, following the sound of the barking dog. Sharp thorns scraped his arms and he could feel the sting from large clumps of nettles around his ankles, but he didn't slow down.

"MORLEY," he cried, panting heavily.

The barking had stopped, but he could still hear him growling. Just ahead he could see Morley's rear half tugging vigorously at something. The something was squealing loudly. It sounded like a small pig. He stepped closer, peering around the brambles that covered the ground.

There was Morley, his jaws clamped tightly around a large and hairy foot. The large and hairy foot was attached to a small scrawny leg, and the small scrawny leg was attached to a body which was halfway inside a hollow tree trunk. Barnaby didn't need to see the top half of the figure to know what Morley had caught. He knew a bogle when he saw one.

# CHAPTER 18
# Ptolemy Tatty

Barnaby grabbed hold of the other skinny leg and hauled the still-squealing young bogle out of the hollow tree. His round body was covered with a ripped tunic that hooked over one shoulder. Thick hairs sprouted from the top of his head like a spiky pineapple, and though it was obvious that he wasn't fully grown, several short whiskers still poked out from his chin. He looked like a miniature caveman.

"Let me go," screeched the little creature. "Let me go."

"Morley," said Barnaby, still keeping a tight

grip on the bogle's other leg. "Leave!"

The little dog reluctantly released the hairy foot, but continued to growl quietly.

"Get that whisker-fink away from me," squealed the bogle, looking fearfully at Morley.

"Whisker – what?" said Barnaby.

"The whisker-fink," he squawked, pointing at the dog, "*that* whisker-fink."

Barnaby looked down at Morley

"If you try to run away," he said, "my whisker-fink will catch you again."

"I won't run away, I promise," the bogle wailed.

Barnaby kept a close eye on him as he quietened Morley down and slowly let go of his leg. The little bogle didn't take his eyes off the dog.

At that moment Granny Hogsflesh came crashing through the bracken. Her red face gleamed alarmingly when she spotted the bogle.

"So, we *were* being followed," she bellowed. "Who are you, and what do you want?"

The bogle slowly got to his feet. So did Barnaby, ready to grab him if he tried to escape. He was extremely small, and didn't even come up to Barnaby's shoulder.

"My name is Ptolemy Tatty," he announced, puffing his chest out, "from the fierce and proud Tatty bogles."

"Well, Tatty whatever your name is—" began Barnaby.

"Ptolemy," he said. "It's spelt with a silent P."

"I don't care how you spell it," said Granny, "I want to know why you were following us."

"P-T-O-L-E-M-Y," he spelt out, "It's pronounced Tol-em-ee. It means warlike."

Barnaby had never seen anyone less warlike than the tiny bogle standing in front of him.

"All the Tatty bogles are warlike, of course," said Ptolemy, "and I am certainly one of the fiercest. So just bear that in mind next time you set your whisker-fink on me. You're lucky I didn't…"

Morley started growling again and Ptolemy covered his head with his arms.

"He can't get you," said Barnaby. "I've got hold of his collar."

"Good, lucky for him that you have," he said,

peeping out from behind his fingers. "Because I would have wrestled him to the ground, and then I would have … wrestled him a bit more and then … um … goodness knows what I would have done. Because I am a fierce and proud Tatty bogle and—"

"You've already said that," interrupted Barnaby.

"Well then," continued the little bogle, "you had better be careful how you treat me, because I could … I could…"

"Talk us to death?" asked Granny.

"Talking is not something bogles do a lot of," said Ptolemy, "especially the Tattys. We are more the strong silent types, not like the Ballybogs, they talk a bit more, but my great-grandmother, Windianna, was a Ballybog, so between you and me, I do like to have a chat now and then, in fact I'm always getting told off by my mother for talking too much, but I can't seem to stop, especially when I'm nervous. But I'm not nervous at all now, not even a bit nervous, which is why I'm being so silent – strong and silent, just like a Tatty Bo—"

"QUIET!" yelled Granny, making both Ptolemy and Barnaby jump. "Why are you following us?"

"I wasn't," he squeaked. "I was just gathering caterpillar cocoons – the grubs inside are delicious." He pulled a large oak leaf out of his pocket and opened it up to reveal several small, delicate sacks. "Want one?"

"No, I do not want one," bellowed Granny. "You have been following us. Admit it."

Ptolemy's face turned a lighter shade of mauve, and he swallowed loudly.

"OK, OK," he said, "I've been trying to get a glimpse of Barnaby for ages – in the house, in the factory tunnel, and now, in the forest." He held up the hem of his ripped tunic. "When I was in your house, your whisker-fink tore a piece off my smock."

"So I wasn't seeing things," said Barnaby. "It was a bogle. But why are you following me?"

"I found out that I had a human relative," he explained, "and I wanted to see what you looked like. We are third cousins."

He grinned timidly up at Barnaby and Granny. "Cousin Barnaby and Aunty Beatrix," he said.

Granny flinched. She wasn't used to hearing her first name.

"Don't call me that," she snapped. "It's Mrs *Ho-flay* to you."

Ptolemy's grin froze on his face.

"Now, you listen to me, you horrible bog-breathed thing," she continued.

Barnaby felt this was slightly unfair coming

from Granny, but said nothing.

"You've been spying on us all this time, so you could kidnap my daughter – his mother." She pointed at Barnaby.

Ptolemy's eyes widened and he shook his head vigorously.

"No, I just wanted to see what you looked like," he said.

Granny took a step closer and he shrank against the tree.

"Where's my daughter?" she said. "What have you done with her?"

"I d-don't know what you're talking about," said Ptolemy.

Granny picked him up by his grubby tunic and held him level with her face.

"Liar!" she hissed. Her face began to contort and Barnaby heard the beginnings of a huge rumble deep inside her vast belly. He knew what was coming and turned away, unable to watch as she released the dampest, gassiest belch, right into Ptolemy's horrified face. His mauve skin turned a green shade of grey, and everything from his hair to his ears drooped. Barnaby almost felt sorry for him.

"Please," he spluttered, "don't do that. I'll tell you anything – anything."

# CHAPTER 19
# Never Trust a Bogle

Granny set a pale Ptolemy down on his feet.

"I'm used to burping," he gasped. "Bogles do it all the time, but I've never experienced anything like that before – ever."

"My daughter has been taken by bogles," said Granny, "and I want to know where she is."

"I swear, I don't know anything about it," said Ptolemy.

Granny took a step towards him again.

"B-but I can help you find her," he added quickly. "I can take you down to Bogle Bog."

"I was banished from your world, many years

ago," said Granny. "So I can't enter Bogle Bog via the swamp. You will have to help us get in another way."

"That's easy," he said. "I was heading there when your whisker-fink caught me."

"Heading where?" asked Granny.

Ptolemy pointed to the tree behind him.

"It's hollow," he said. "It leads to a huge ladder that reaches all the way down to Bogle Bog. It's only supposed to be used as an exit as it's very hard to pass others on the ladder, but sometimes I use it in emergencies."

"Of course," cried Barnaby. "Mum and I used it last time we were here. Why didn't we think of that before?"

Granny nodded slowly.

"Yes, I remember the ladder," she said. "Barnaby, get the dog to guard the bogle. We need to talk privately."

Barnaby sat Morley down in front of the nervous Ptolemy and walked over to Granny, who had moved some distance away.

"Bogles are terrified of dogs, or 'whisker-finks', as they call them," she explained. "They can sneak around humans and cause mischief undetected, but a dog will always sniff them out. We can use Morley to our advantage."

Barnaby nodded.

"Are we going to trust him," he asked, "and go down the ladder?"

"No, we're not going to trust him," said Granny. "But I think the hollow tree is our only option. I'll go first, then the bogle, then you follow on with Morley."

They walked over to Ptolemy. He and Morley were still staring at each other warily.

"OK, we've decided to go with you," said Granny. "But any funny business and I'll set the whisker-fink on you."

"No funny business, I promise," he said.

They made their way over to the hollow tree.

"I really want to help you find your mother," said Ptolemy to Barnaby, as Granny peered down into the tree. "We're cousins. You can trust me."

Barnaby looked down at the small figure. His dad's last words were still ringing loudly in his ears as two large dark eyes blinked up at him – never trust a bogle.

# CHAPTER 20
# Trapped

Granny Hogsflesh climbed into the hole in the hollow tree and slowly lowered herself down.

"It's a bit snug," she said.

Barnaby walked around the trunk, judging its size. It looked smaller than Granny.

"I think you should come out," he said. "Maybe we need to think about this more carefully."

"What do you mean?" said Granny, squeezing herself lower in.

"I think you may be too big," he said, regretting it immediately.

Granny's silvery skin started glowing.

"I am not too big," she puffed. "The tree is too small."

"That's what I meant," said Barnaby, hastily. "So climb out and we'll have another think."

Granny's top half was still poking out of the tree. She grabbed hold of a nearby root and tried to haul her great frame out of the trunk. Her gleaming face turned as purple as her hat as she strained and pulled. The hollow tree started to sway dangerously.

"She's going to uproot the whole thing," cried Ptolemy. "Quick! Dive for cover."

He shot into the undergrowth, but was soon dragged back by a growling Morley, who was tugging vigorously on the hem of Ptolemy's smock.

"Bad whisker-fink," he shouted, "naughty whisker-fink."

"You're not going anywhere," grunted

Barnaby, reaching for Granny's hands and pulling with all his might. "I bet you knew this was going to happen."

"I didn't," cried Ptolemy. "Here, let me help you."

He stood behind Barnaby, put his arms around his waist and began pulling. Morley joined in too and tugged the back of Ptolemy's clothes as hard as he could. But it was no good. The three of them could not pull Granny out of the tree.

"STOP!" she shrieked. "You're ruining my silk gloves."

They all let go and fell on to the leafy ground.

"We could try to push her down," suggested Ptolemy.

Granny glared up at him.

"You silly bird-brained bogle," she said. "Do you want to ruin my hat too?"

Ptolemy stared at the long purple feather

that sprang from Granny's tiny hat and absent-mindedly pinged it with his long bony finger. Granny slapped his hand away and he squealed and backed off.

"Let's all just calm down and think," said Barnaby. "Granny, can you move in any direction?"

"No," she puffed. "Nowhere."

"Then we're going to need something to make you slippery," said Barnaby. "Like soap or oil."

"What's soap?"

Barnaby looked down at the tatty little bogle and wrinkled his nose.

"It's something that you could do with," he said, "and lots of it."

"Pass me my pickle bag," said Granny. "There may be something in there that could help us."

Barnaby hauled the big bag closer and started to unload its contents. He read out each label.

"Free-range turkey trumps?" he asked.

Granny shook her head.

"Selected worm burps?"

"No," she said.

"Beetroot?"

Granny thought for a moment.

"Useful in many situations," she said, "but unfortunately not this one."

Barnaby heaved the heaviest jar out of the sack.

"And there's the rhino sneeze, of course," he said. "But you can't use that. You said it still had the cold virus encased in it."

Barnaby began to pack it away.

"Wait," said Granny. "Mucus is slippery."

"But you can't," said Barnaby. "You would have to rub it all over yourself."

Granny said nothing, but nodded grimly.

"You can't," he repeated. "It will give you the worst cold ever, and besides —" he shook the jar, wobbling its green slimy contents "— look at it."

"I think it looks nice," said Ptolemy. "Can I have a go?"

Barnaby ignored him and slowly unscrewed the big round lid. He turned away as a thick vapour escaped from the open jar and the stench of sickness drifted out.

"Quick," shouted Granny. "Push it closer towards me and then stand clear."

Barnaby did as he was told, then watched as she took a deep breath and plunged her hand into the viscous jelly.

# CHAPTER 21
# Rhino Sneeze

Slowly but determinedly Granny covered her top half in the green rhino sneeze. As she did, her long nose lost its silvery sheen and turned red. Barnaby took a step forward.

"Keep back," she said. "There's no point in us both catching a – a – a – tishoo – a cold."

Ptolemy appeared to be enjoying the whole thing, and was skipping around the hollow tree.

"I want to be covered in green slime too," he said.

"This isn't a game," said Barnaby, angrily. "Are you OK, Granny?"

Her skin and clothes were now covered in the thick goo.

"My nose is running," she croaked, "my eyes are streaming, and my dress is dry-clean only. Of course I'm not OK!"

Ptolemy had stopped dancing around the tree, but a big smile had spread across his hairy little face as he looked down at the slimy Granny. Barnaby caught his eye and he quickly replaced the smile with a look of concern.

"Poor Aunty Beatrix," he said.

Granny's bloodshot eyes swivelled sharply up at him.

"You will address me as Mrs *Ho-flay*," she sniffed.

Ptolemy's ears drooped.

"You're pretty much covered now, Granny," said Barnaby. "See if you can move."

Granny got hold of the root and tried to haul

herself up again.

"It's no good," she panted. "My top half is slippery, but my bottom half isn't. I can't reach it with the rhino sneeze."

"Why don't you try pushing instead of pulling?" suggested Ptolemy.

"I don't need advice from you," snorted Granny. "ATISHOO!"

"It might not be a bad idea to push," said Barnaby. "See if your legs can reach the bogle ladder."

Granny wedged her hands against the inside of the tree and started to push herself down. Very slowly she began to disappear inside.

"It's working," she cried. "I'm moving."

Barnaby felt so relieved that he almost hugged Ptolemy.

"Thank goodness," he said. "Keep pushing."

Granny's head completely vanished inside

the hollow tree and only the long purple feather from her hat poked out of the hole.

"I can feel the ladder with my toes," boomed Granny's voice from below.

"Great," shouted Barnaby.

He turned to Ptolemy. "Now, you're going next, but I'll be right behind you, so don't try anything stupid."

"Why would I?" said Ptolemy. "I want to help you."

"I'll believe that when I see it," said Barnaby. "Right, in you go."

Ptolemy backed into the hollow tree and lowered himself down. There was a yell from inside.

"He's on my head," shouted Granny's muffled voice. "Get that thing off my hat."

Ptolemy leapt out of the hole.

"She's still down there," he squawked. "I didn't mean to stand on her silly hat."

"It most definitely is *not* a silly hat," came the angry cry from below. "And if you've squashed it, then I'll squash you."

Ptolemy's face turned pale.

"I'm sorry," he called down the hole. "It was an accident."

"Never mind the hat," said Barnaby. "What's going on down there? Are you stuck again?"

"Never mind the hat?" screamed Granny. "Never mind the hat?"

There was a moment of silence.

"The tree is too small!" she announced.

Barnaby slumped down on to the forest floor and put his head in his hands.

"Now what?" he sighed.

"We could try and poke her down with a stick," suggested Ptolemy.

"I do not require a poking stick," yelled the voice from the hole.

They sat in silence for a moment.

"I know," cried Ptolemy, jumping to his feet. "I will go down to Bogle Bog the normal way, through the swamp. Then I can climb the ladder and pull her out from the other end."

"No way," said Barnaby. "You would just run off."

Ptolemy sat down again. To Barnaby's surprise, he covered his face with his hands and began to cry.

"You don't understand," he sniffed. "I would never run off, because you're all I have."

Barnaby felt uncomfortable. He didn't like to see anyone crying, but he knew not to trust Ptolemy.

"You don't even know me," he said. "What are you talking about?"

"I'm an orphan," he sobbed, "and just like you, I don't have any brothers or sisters. That's why I came to find you. You're the only family that I have."

"I don't believe you," said Barnaby. "You said earlier that your mother was always telling you off for talking too much."

The crying stopped and Ptolemy looked at Barnaby from between his fingers.

"What I meant," he said, "was that, *apart* from my mother, I'm an orphan."

"That doesn't make sense," said Barnaby, angrily. "You're a liar."

"No, I'm not," cried Ptolemy. "I just meant that I'm a sibling orphan – no brothers or sisters – just like you."

"Being an only child is very different from being an orphan!" shouted Barnaby.

Ptolemy lowered his hands. His cheeks were dry, but he did look upset.

"OK, so I'm not a complete orphan," he sniffed. "But I did lose my father, Fumacious

Tatty, to Marsh Fever about a year ago. My mother, Gasienna, came from Bogle Bog before she married him and moved away to live with the Tattys. After his death she wanted to move back. So I haven't been there that long and I haven't got many friends or anything. That's why I was curious about you." Ptolemy stared down at the ground. "I just thought we could be like brothers," he said in a small voice.

Barnaby had always wanted a brother, but definitely not a bogle one.

"Cousins is bad enough," he said, standing up.

Granny's voice floated out of the hollow tree.

"This is all very touching," she called, "but my legs are dangling down into Bogle Bog. We need to do something quickly."

Barnaby pulled Ptolemy up to his feet.

"OK, Bogle Bog it is," he said. "But I'm coming with you."

# CHAPTER 22

# The Swamp

Barnaby crouched beside the hollow tree. The tip of Granny's hat feather popped out and tickled his knees.

"Did you hear that, Granny?" he called down. "We are going to try and pull you out from the other side."

"I heard," she said. "I don't like it, but there doesn't seem to be any other way, and it's getting rather hot in here."

"I'll be fine, don't worry," he said. "I've got Morley to protect me."

Ptolemy looked down at the excited dog, who

was now running in circles around the tree.

"Oh no," he said. "No no no. Absolutely no whisker-finks allowed in Bogle Bog."

Barnaby got to his feet.

"Well, *this* whisker-fink is coming with me," he said.

"You can't," said Ptolemy. "We have to sneak through the village and climb up the ladder without being noticed. A whisker-fink will cause widespread panic."

"He's right," called Granny, from down below. "You'll have to leave Morley with me."

Barnaby caught hold of Morley's collar and sat him down beside the tree. He was feeling very uneasy. It had been Ptolemy's idea to go through the tree, even though Granny was clearly too big. And now he wouldn't let Morley come with them, and Barnaby would be on his own. It felt like a trap, but he had no choice.

"You stay here, boy," he said, stroking Morley's silky ears.

The little dog started whining.

"It's OK, don't cry. Granny's just down there," he said, pointing towards the hole, "and I promise I won't be long."

"You better not be," shouted Granny. "I'm beginning to lose all feeling in my bottom."

Barnaby gave Morley a final pat.

"I'll be as quick as I can, Granny," he called. "Just hang in there."

"I *am* hanging," she yelled.

"Come on, then," said Barnaby to a grinning Ptolemy. "Let's go."

They made their way through the thick forest. Barnaby could just make out a clearing up ahead of them. The smell of decaying vegetation and wet animal waste drifted through the trees.

Ptolemy inhaled deeply.

"Ah," he sighed, "the sweet smell of the bog."

Barnaby hid his nose down his jumper. The terrible stench reminded him of the last time he'd been here, almost one year ago, when he and his mum had jumped into the swamp to save his dad, and were dragged down into the bogle underworld. He was sure Ptolemy could hear his heart hammering as they walked into the clearing and stood before the stinking sludge.

"This is the best thing about living in Bogle Bog," said Ptolemy, happily. "The swamp. I haven't been to many places, but I can't imagine anywhere more beautiful. I would like to travel, though, maybe visit distant Tatty relatives. Did I mention that I'm from the fierce and proud Tatty Bogle clan? I think I might have done, but the thing is, I would always like to come back here again because…"

Ptolemy carried on talking and talking. Barnaby tried to block him out, and looked around at the putrid swamp. A low toxic mist lay on the surface and tangled dead trees fell into the surrounding edges. He glanced down at the greeny-brown gunge immediately in front of him. Every so often, acrid air bubbles belched up from below.

"The view, the smell," continued Ptolemy, sniffing the air, "everything about it is just … well, it's hard to put into words, but I'll try—"

"No, don't," said Barnaby. "Please, just stop talking for one minute. I can't stand it any more. I thought bogles were supposed to be surly, silent creatures."

"I am surly and silent," said Ptolemy indignantly, "very surly and very silent; fierce, proud and warlike, of course. But the thing is, I like you, cousin Barnaby."

"Don't call me that," snapped Barnaby. "I do not want to be here, with you, jumping into that." He gestured towards the bog. "I can't even swim. I'm here because I have to save my mum. So let's just get this over with."

Ptolemy nodded solemnly and jumped in with both feet.

"You don't have to be able to swim," he called. He was up to his knees in the bog, but quickly started sinking down. "Come on. What are you waiting for? It's lovely once you get in."

Barnaby tried to reply, but his mouth was so dry, no sound came out. He closed his eyes, held his nose, and jumped.

# CHAPTER 23

# The Journey Underground

Barnaby sank down into the bog. The cold mud oozed up over his legs, quickly reaching his waist. Ptolemy was already completely submerged, a small pool of bubbles the only sign of where he had been. The brown slush squelched hungrily up Barnaby's body. He knew it was pointless to struggle, but he couldn't stop himself. The freezing bog was swallowing him whole, rising up around his neck and filling his ears with thick black sludge. He managed to crane his neck up and take a final gulp of stinking boggy air before being dragged completely under.

Barnaby held his breath and shut his eyes tightly as he was sucked ever deeper inside the swamp. He could feel the dense slime sliding over his body, covering his face, filling his nostrils, squashing his lungs until there was nothing left inside them. But just as he felt his chest was about to rupture, there was a loud pop, and an air bubble opened out around his head. He gasped for breath, coughing and sneezing the mud from his nose, but the relief didn't last. The sucking got stronger and his journey got faster. A sudden drop made his stomach flip and churn as he was pulled round and down into the depths of the earth. His body was jerked from side to side until eventually he flew out of a hole high in a rock face, through the air, and landed on his bottom in a thick pile of soft moss.

He lay there for a moment, winded and dazed,

and blinked up at the high muddy roof way above him. Tree roots poked out of the ceiling like giant spider legs. He was in a vast underground cavern, ten times the size of the Hogsflesh Pickle Company.

"Bogle Bog," he muttered to himself. "I can't believe I'm here again."

"Believe it," said a voice.

He turned to see Ptolemy coming towards him, his grubby little face glowing with excitement.

"How was your ride through the swamp?" he asked. "Isn't it the best fun?"

Barnaby slowly got to his feet.

"No," he said, rubbing his bottom. "It's the worst. I hate it."

"I can tell you're part bogle, Mr Grumpy," said Ptolemy, cheerfully.

Barnaby sighed. He was beginning to prefer the surly, silent bogles to the chirpy, chatty ones.

"Anyway, I told you I wouldn't run off,"

Ptolemy continued, "and here I am, ready to help. We have to make our way through the village without being noticed, and at the moment, we are right in the middle of the Landing Square. Hide behind this rock while we think of the best way of getting to the ladder."

Barnaby squatted behind a large boulder and peered over the top at the village. It often appeared in his nightmares and was just as he remembered it – dark, smelly and hot. Burning lanterns lined the winding gravel paths, dimly lighting up the perfectly round mud houses. Most had two or three spherical rooms attached to the main ball. The houses around him were arranged to form three sides of a large square. The fourth was the rock face with the holes in, which they had just shot out of. Although he had been here before, he didn't know it was called the Landing Square, but he could see why. Several large beds of moss were strategically placed to catch the falling bogles as they shot out of the holes above.

Barnaby's entrance seemed to have gone unnoticed. He could just make out the small dark shapes of bogles walking the streets and going about their business.

He shuddered and crouched lower as one of them walked towards them holding a walking stick. Barnaby looked around for Ptolemy, but he had gone. He was greeting the other bogle and leading him towards Barnaby's hiding place. The bogle was ancient – he looked much older than Granny. His spiky grey hair framed his scowling face like a chimney sweep's brush.

"Well?" he grunted. "Did you do it?"

"Yes, Uncle," said Ptolemy, pointing towards the boulder. "Over here."

Barnaby's heart stopped. It was a trap, and he had fallen right into it.

# CHAPTER 24

# Disguise

Barnaby crouched behind the big boulder, listening to the approaching footsteps.

"Did you get them?" asked the old bogle.

"I could only get one," said Ptolemy. "It was really tricky. You should come with me next time I go above ground, Uncle. The bog is really beautiful at this time of year and—"

"Ptolemy!" said the decrepit bogle. "Remember, bogles should never chitter-chat. Speak only when necessary and practise your scowling more."

"Yes, of course," said Ptolemy. "I am trying

my best, Uncle, it's just that I'm a bit excited."

Barnaby looked around frantically. They had nearly reached the boulder. His only chance was to push past them and make a run for it. He had a vague idea of where the long ladder was that reached up to the roof of the enormous cavern. But Granny was plugging up the hole in the hollow tree. Would he be able to pull her out in time? The bogles were almost on top of him. He had to pick the right moment.

"I have been very silent and surly today," continued Ptolemy. "In fact, 'Silence' could be my middle name – not that I have a middle name – but if I did then it would definitely be 'Silence', or maybe even 'Surly'. Both would suit me, just like 'Ptolemy' suits me because I'm so war—"

"Just show me what you've got," interrupted the old bogle.

Barnaby took a deep breath, ready to spring

out from behind the boulder.

"One caterpillar cocoon," said Ptolemy, unwrapping the leaf on top of the rock, "and several fat juicy earthworms."

Barnaby slumped down, relief flooding his body.

"Hmm," said the old bogle, stuffing a worm into his mouth. "Not great, but I suppose it will have to do. Next time, see if you can find some maggots. I'll squeeze them and make us some juice. "

"Yum! Thank you, Uncle," said Ptolemy, as the elderly bogle walked off.

Barnaby listened as his footsteps faded. A minute later Ptolemy's head appeared above him.

"It's all right," he said, "he's gone."

Barnaby peered over the top just in time to see the bogle disappear down one of the winding streets.

"I told you I was looking for caterpillar cocoons," said Ptolemy. "That was another relative of ours, but I thought you might not want to be introduced."

Barnaby closed his eyes and waited for his pounding heart to return to normal.

"Now, if you want to get through the village without causing a fuss," Ptolemy went on, "we're going to have to disguise you as a bogle. That smooth chin will never do, and you're far too clean."

Barnaby looked down at his clothes. Despite being swallowed up by the bog, there wasn't a mark on them.

"The swamp never leaves a mess," explained Ptolemy. "All the wet sludge is blasted off you with the force of the drop."

At that moment an enormous globule of bog fell from the high ceiling and landed on top of

his head, splattering his face and jumper. "That's better," said Ptolemy. "But what can we do with that gruesome chin?"

"My chin's not gruesome," cried Barnaby.

Ptolemy pulled a face.

"Takes a bit of getting used to," he said. "We'll have to cover it up."

He looked around for something suitable.

"There's nothing here but mud and moss," said Barnaby.

"Perfect!" grinned Ptolemy, picking up a gooey handful of soft mud and slapping it on to Barnaby's chin.

"Hey," cried Barnaby. "Stop that."

Ptolemy looked up impatiently.

"Do you want to get through this village unnoticed or not?" he said.

"Yes, but—"

"Well, get sticking then," he said, handing him bits of green moss. "The moss will stick to the mud as it dries to your chin."

"A moss beard?" asked Barnaby. "It will look ridiculous."

"Unless you can think of another idea," said Ptolemy, "or you can grow a beard in the next five minutes, then it's going to have to do."

Barnaby sighed and began sticking the pieces of moss on to his muddy chin. It was very uncomfortable and started itching immediately. When all the moss had been attached, Ptolemy stood back and looked at him.

"Hmm," he muttered. "It's not great, but

better than nothing. You're just going to have to keep your head down, and if we get stopped, let me do all the talking."

They emerged from behind the rock and walked along one of the gravel paths, dodging the splats of bog that continually dropped from the high ceiling above. Barnaby kept his head down, glad that the burning lamps didn't give out much light.

He wasn't sure if it was the heat or the anxiety that was making the sweat pour from his forehead, but it was running down his face and dislodging pieces of fake beard. They trudged through the narrow streets, keeping to the shadows to avoid large groups of bogles.

"Nearly there," whispered Ptolemy. "That was easy, wasn't it?"

Barnaby could just make out the long ladder a little way ahead of them.

"Yes, great," he said. "I'll go up first and see if I can pull Granny down."

"I'll keep a lookout," said Ptolemy as they came to the bottom of the huge ladder.

Barnaby looked up and could just make out Granny's fat legs dangling down from the cavern ceiling like a pair of large water balloons. He swallowed and put a shaky foot on the first rung. He didn't like heights.

"Ptolemy?" cried a squeaky voice behind them. "Are you going up above ground?"

Barnaby turned to see a short squat female with curly blonde whiskers poking out from her pointy chin.

"I'm on my way too," she said. "Who's your friend?"

Barnaby slowly climbed down and backed off into the shadows. Now what were they going to do?

# CHAPTER 25
## Bearditis

"Hello, Grubbiana," said Ptolemy. "This is my ... um ... cousin."

The bogle girl peered through the gloom at Barnaby.

"A Tatty cousin?" she asked.

"Yes, yes, a Tatty cousin," said Ptolemy. "Barna ... beard Tatty."

"Hello, Barnabeard," she said, taking a step closer.

Barnaby grunted and tried to look away, but she was right beside him, studying his face.

"What's wrong with his beard?" she gasped, backing off quickly. "It's green."

Ptolemy looked sadly at Barnaby.

"Bearditis," he said solemnly. "It's still very infectious."

The bogle girl grasped her own curly whiskers and started edging away.

"He shouldn't be allowed out in that state," she said. "He could spark an outbreak. Get him out of here."

"I am," said Ptolemy. "Are you still coming?"

But she had already disappeared down one of the gravel paths.

Ptolemy grinned as Barnaby stepped out of the shadows and climbed back on to the ladder.

"Nothing like a bit of bearditis to keep people away," he chuckled. "Actually, it's no laughing matter. Another relative of ours caught it once, a long time ago, and was terribly ill. But it's the shame that's the worst bit. The B-word – baldness. Some bogles think it's unlucky to mention the B-word, but I think if you say something enough times then it makes it less scary – bald, balding, baldy…"

Barnaby started to climb as Ptolemy chuntered on. He closed his eyes and concentrated on putting one hand and one foot above the other.

"My uncle – actually he's a great, great, great uncle – doesn't mind using the word 'bald', but then again he wouldn't, would he, being a 'Baldric' and all. Strange name to give a bogle, if you ask me – not that anyone ever does ask me. But if they did, then I think…"

Ptolemy's voice got fainter and fainter the higher Barnaby climbed. After a couple of minutes a purple suede shoe banged into the top of his head.

"Aaatishooooooo!" came a muffled sneeze from above.

"Granny?" he called.

"Is that you, Barnaby?" she yelled. "You took

your time. I have pins and needles in places I didn't think were possible."

"I'm sorry," he shouted. "I came as quickly as I could. Now, I'm going to hang on to your leg and pull you out. Get ready."

He nervously let go of the ladder with one hand and grabbed hold of Granny's thick ankle, giving it a gentle tug. Nothing happened.

"You're going to have to pull harder than that," came the voice from above.

Barnaby's palms were sweating as he looked down at the bogle village way below. He wiped them on his trousers and wrapped his hand as far as he could around Granny's chunky leg and pulled with all his might. Granny's body lurched downwards about thirty centimetres, jerking Barnaby right off the ladder. He yelled as he swung out over the tiny mud houses far below. He could hear Granny's muffled screams above him.

"What are you doing?" she shrieked.

Barnaby couldn't speak. But he managed to grasp hold of Granny's other ankle with his spare hand. He knew he had to get his feet back on to the ladder and tried to swing towards it, not daring to look down.

"AAARRRGGGHHH!" screeched Granny, as her bottom half swung from side to side like a giant pendulum. "What's going on down there?"

Barnaby's foot reached the ladder and he managed to tuck it under a rung just as he felt the roof above him rumble.

"I'M GOING," she screamed from overhead. "I'M SLIPPING!"

Barnaby had one hand on the ladder, the other still around Granny's ankle, when an avalanche of mud, roots and grandmother toppled over him. His hand slipped and his stomach lurched as he plummeted down towards the hard ground.

# CHAPTER 26
# The Bog-Smog

Barnaby had heard stories about people's lives flashing in front of them just before they died. He had never really believed it before, but as he hurtled towards the earth far below, still holding on to his grandmother's ankle, time seemed to slow down. Images of his mum and dad in the little house where he grew up flashed through his mind, followed by Granny in her mansion, Hogsflesh Pickles and finally Bogle Bog.

He almost felt calm as the ground raced towards him, and he closed his eyes, ready for the crunch of his bones and the squish of his neck as his grandmother landed on top of him. But instead of a crash, the arm that was still firmly grasping Granny's leg was almost torn from its socket as their fall came to an abrupt end. He lost his grip and fell the remaining two metres to the ground with a thud.

Barnaby looked up to see Granny clinging to the ladder just above him. She had managed to grasp hold of it, breaking their fall. She climbed down the remaining rungs and adjusted her hat, which was still pinned firmly to her head.

"Stupid boy!" she puffed. "What were you trying to do up there? You could have knocked my hat off."

"Sorry, Granny," he panted, "I was just trying to—"

"Lucky for you," she interrupted, "that I'm a member of the Senior Ladies' Trapeze Society. AAATISHOOO!"

Barnaby didn't know what to say and just stared at her open-mouthed.

"And what's that ridiculous thing on your chin?" she asked, examining his face.

"It's my bogle beard," he said defensively, patting the few remaining pieces of moss.

"You look like you're being attacked by a savage lawn," she said, walking past him and looking around. "Oh my goodness – Bogle Bog." Granny sighed and wiped her nose on a monogrammed handkerchief. "I never thought I would set foot in this place again. It hasn't changed a bit."

Ptolemy appeared from behind them.

"Ah, there you are," he said, apparently unaware of the drama that had just occurred. "That was quick."

Granny looked him up and down.

"You're still here, then," she said, through

pursed lips.

"Yes, Aunty Bea … I mean, Mrs *Ho-flay*," he said. "Have you got the whisker-fink with you?"

"The whisker-fink is still waiting by the hollow tree, not that it's any of your business," said Granny. "I don't intend to be in this stinking place for very long. We're going to find my daughter and go. Now, where shall we start?"

She looked expectantly at Ptolemy, who took a step back.

"I don't know," he said. "I told you that I could help you get into Bogle Bog, but I don't know where she is – honest."

Just then, two hairy bogles crunched up the gravel path towards them. They stared suspiciously at Granny and Barnaby.

"Where are you going, Ptolemy? And who are they?" asked one of them, pointing rudely.

"I'm not going anywhere … and, um … not

doing anything," said Ptolemy, as Granny and Barnaby stepped back into the darkness. "And these are just some ... um ... visiting Tatty cousins."

"Tatty bogles?" said the other one, glaring at Barnaby through the gloom. He was much bigger and wider than Ptolemy. His face twisted in a permanent scowl and his thick whiskers shot out randomly. "I suppose they are fierce and warlike, just like you," he said, pushing Ptolemy to the ground.

The second bogle laughed a horrible, high-pitched hyena cackle.

"C'mon, Musty," he said, walking towards the ladder and flicking Ptolemy's nose as he passed. "Let's leave the *ferocious* Tattys and find some humans to annoy."

Barnaby held his breath as the one called Musty continued to stare at him.

"What's wrong with your beard?" he asked, suspiciously.

Barnaby heard Granny clear her throat, followed by a loud, "BBRRRAAAAAPPPPP!"

The bogle's knees sagged as he stood in the veil of Granny's belch. Then he staggered backwards to the foot of the ladder.

"Evacuate!" he called to his friend, who had already started to climb. "Tatty burps are toxic."

Barnaby breathed out sharply as he watched them go, blowing a piece of mossy beard from his chin.

"Get rid of that ridiculous stuff on your face," said Granny. "It's attracting too much attention."

He peeled off the remnants of his fake beard as Ptolemy got to his feet and dusted himself off.

"It can be hard being a Tatty," he said, glancing

up at the ladder. "Everyone is scared of you – even your friends."

"Those were your friends?" asked Barnaby, incredulously.

"Kind of," mumbled Ptolemy, fidgeting with his smock. "I don't really have any friends, being a Tatty bogle and everything. But at least they talk to me, so that sort of counts as friends, doesn't it?"

Barnaby suddenly felt sorry for Ptolemy. He knew what it was like to be an outsider.

"Anyway," continued Ptolemy, "it's not safe to talk here. Let's go somewhere quieter."

He led them through the dark streets to the edge of the village. They were at the far end of the huge cavern. The round houses petered out, giving way to a rocky expanse covered in a low mist. A large area was cordoned off by a tall fence made of wooden poles with spikes on top, and two enormous gates to one side. As they made their way towards it, Barnaby felt the temperature drop.

"I didn't know you could get mist underground," he said.

He peered at one of the poles and was shocked to see hundreds of tiny bogle faces carved into the smooth surface.

"It's always misty here," said Ptolemy. "We call it bog-smog. Vapours from rotting swamp plants mix with the fog above ground and sink through the marshes, settling here."

"Smells like it," said Barnaby, screwing up his nose and examining one of the chiselled faces in the fence pole. He looked round at Granny. She was standing a few paces back, her red nose shining like a beacon.

"What is this place?" he asked.

"The Bogle Burial Ground," she whispered.

# CHAPTER 27
# Gates to the Graveyard

Barnaby peered between the carved poles into the Bogle Burial Ground. Rows of jagged rocks loomed up out of the cold mist that skimmed the ground. He could just make out symbols chiselled into the surface of them, but was too far away to see exactly what they were. He glanced round at Granny, who had moved away and was now standing before the two enormous and intricately engraved wooden gates. She beckoned him over.

"Look," she said, running her hand down one of the tall gateposts. It too was covered in tiny chiselled bogles. Each twisted wooden face looked scarier than the next.

"These are to ward off evil spirits," explained Granny. "My parents will be buried in this graveyard."

Barnaby looked through the gates at the ominous grey stones dipped in the cold fog. He didn't like this place, and wanted to leave as soon as possible.

"I want to visit their graves," Granny said in a low voice.

Barnaby's heart sank.

"You can't do that," said Ptolemy from behind them. "Only the Bogle Elders are allowed in.

"Well, you can't get much more elderly than me," said Granny.

"But it's forbidden," he said. "If they catch you, you'll get us all cursed with the bog-smog."

"What's that?" asked Barnaby.

"The curse of the bog-smog makes the mist follow you wherever you go," said Ptolemy, looking around him as he spoke. "You can never get away from it. Your own personal little cloud surrounds you for ever."

"That's terrible," said Barnaby, sniffing the air. "It stinks."

"That's not the problem," said Ptolemy. "I think it smells nice. It's the cold it brings with it. It will chill you to the bone, and one thing bogles hate is being cold."

"AAATISHOOOO! And one thing I hate is having a cold," said Granny, dabbing her crimson nose. "But bogle curses don't scare me." She began rattling the gates. "And if I want to visit my parents' graves, then I will."

"I don't want anything to do with this," Ptolemy said, backing away from them. "I'm sorry, Barnaby, I really did want to help you find your mother, but I'm not doing this."

"Ptolemy, wait," cried Barnaby. But the little bogle had turned and fled.

He felt strangely sad as he watched him go.

"Thank goodness he's gone," said Granny. "We don't need him any more."

"He could have helped us," said Barnaby.

"Helped us?" she cried. "You're forgetting what your father told you before we left – never trust a bogle."

"I suppose," he sighed. "But he did help us get this far."

"Hmmph!" she grumbled. "We could have easily got this far without him. Now, help me try and open this gate."

She started to push against the tall wooden frame. Barnaby could hear the gate and surrounding fence creak and groan against her weight.

"Bogle Elders, indeed!" she fumed, ramming her great bulk against it. "Well, they're not going to keep me out."

The huge frame began to bend, and Barnaby was sure he heard a snap.

"Wait," he cried. "You're going to bring the whole thing down."

Granny backed off for a moment and blew her streaming nose on her posh hankie. Barnaby took the opportunity to stand between her and the gate.

"Are you sure this is a good idea, Granny?" he asked. "Shouldn't we be concentrating on finding Mum?"

"Barnaby, if there is one thing that my long life has taught me," she said, tucking her hankie up her sleeve, "it is that when an opportunity presents itself to you, grab it. You never know where it might lead. I have to do this. You see, I never had a chance to say goodbye."

Barnaby nodded slowly.

"OK, I understand," he sighed, pushing the gate. It didn't budge, so he pulled instead, and the great wooden frame swung easily towards him.

"Ah, pull not push," said Granny. "I knew that."

Barnaby took a deep breath as he and his grandmother stepped into the cold bog-smog.

# CHAPTER 28
# The Bogle Burial Ground

As Barnaby and Granny walked into the Bogle Burial Ground, they felt the temperature drop another ten degrees. Barnaby pulled on his jumper and wrapped his arms around his body. The bog-smog was so thick on the ground he could hardly see his legs. He followed Granny towards a large jagged rock. It was inscribed with several weird symbols and a name. Barnaby realized it was, in fact, a tombstone. Granny stooped to read it.

"Gaseous the Great," she said quietly. "He was a great bogle Chieftain who died a long time ago."

Barnaby knelt down to study the stone.

"This is a blackthorn fighting stick," she said, pointing to one of the symbols, "to show that Gaseous was a great warrior. There used to be many battles between the different bogle clans."

"How many clans are there?" asked Barnaby.

"Hundreds," replied Granny. "There are bogles all around the world, although different countries call them different things – the Kobolds of Germany, the Yokai of Japan, the Bogeys of North America…"

Barnaby peered at the engraving. Next to it was a bird.

"What's that," he asked, "a chicken? Why is there a chicken on it?"

Granny stood up, frowning.

"It's not a chicken, you stupid boy," she snapped. "It's a raven – a messenger from this world to the next – or so the bogles believe.

Anyway, we're wasting time here. We're supposed to be looking for my parents' graves. Keep an eye out for the names Baldric and Mary Ballybog."

Barnaby stayed close to Granny as they went from tombstone to tombstone reading the strange inscriptions:

HERE LIES WHIFFRED BOG
AND HIS SCOWLING WIFE SMELLENOR BOG
MAY THEY FESTER IN PEACE

Some of the graves were so old, the carved names were hard to read. They found a Fusty, a Brawler, an Odourus, a Marsha and even a Dave, but no Baldrics or Marys.

"You're stepping on my heels," said Granny, shooing him away. "It will be quicker if we split up."

Barnaby didn't want to stray too far from

Granny. The graveyard, with its strange rocks and mist, made him feel very uneasy. What if they were caught, and cursed with the bog-smog for entering? He glanced nervously at the gates. Just beyond them, on the outside of the burial ground, he noticed another jagged rock. It was close to where they had been standing. It was similar to the

rough tombstones inside and he wondered why he hadn't seen it before, and why it was on the other side of the fence. He left Granny reading each stone and walked out of the large gates. The rock was partly hidden by a large spiky bush, and the front of it was covered in weeds. Barnaby knelt down to get a better look. He carefully parted the tangled mess of thorns. There were no intricate engravings carved into the stone, only a name in plain bold letters.

MARY
BALLYBOG

Barnaby jumped up.

"Granny," he called. "Over here."

A minute later Granny stomped through the gates.

"It's no good," she sighed. "I've checked every tombstone and there's no sign of them."

"I think I might have found your mother," he said.

"You can't have done," she grumbled. "Not out here."

She waddled over, knelt down and parted the barbed twigs of the bush to read the gravestone. She said nothing for a long time and just stared at the plain words.

"Are you OK, Granny?" asked Barnaby.

She swallowed and he could see her eyes were moist.

"I'm fine," she said, "it's just this silly cold."

She took out her hankie and blew her nose.

"They never accepted her," she murmured. "Not even in death."

"What do you mean?"

"As you know, Barnaby, my mother was a human," sniffed Granny. "And it seems that even though she married a bogle and lived here for a long time, they wouldn't even give her a decent burial."

She pulled a clump of weeds out of the ground.

"I suspect we are the first ones to visit this grave," she sighed.

Barnaby looked at Granny. He had the odd sensation of feeling sorry for her. She was normally so loud and bossy.

"I'm sorry," he said.

"No use worrying about the past," she said, standing up and brushing herself down. "It's the present and the future that we should be concentrating on. I hate to admit it, but you were right. We shouldn't have wasted time here. Let's go and find your mother."

"But what about your father's grave?"

"No," she sighed, "come on. I don't want to stay here a minute longer."

They turned to go back towards the way they had come. But just beyond the mist, Barnaby thought he saw a small bogle figure.

"Wait," he said. "I think someone's coming."

They both crouched down behind Granny's mother's tombstone.

"It might be Ptolemy," he whispered, as Granny peeped over the top.

"It's not Ptolemy," she croaked, sinking down on to the ground.

Her eyes were wide with fear and Barnaby felt the hairs on his neck prick up.

"We have to hide," she breathed. "I was right all along... It's Belchetta Ballybog."

# CHAPTER 29
# Hidden

Barnaby started to tremble and he squeezed his knees tight against his chest as he cowered behind his great-grandmother's tombstone, glad of the thick, smelly bog-smog.

"It can't be Belchetta," he whispered. "People don't come back from the dead."

"Get down," hissed Granny, squeezing herself under the thorny bush. She held her finger up to her mouth as footsteps approached. Barnaby squashed himself flat against the back of the tombstone, his breath coming in short spasms.

He glanced over to where Granny lay beneath the spiky bush and was horrified to see the long purple feather of her hat sprouting proudly out of the mist. The footsteps stopped in front of the grave and Barnaby held his breath.

"Good riddance to bad rubbish," the bogle croaked, kicking some dirt up against the gravestone.

Then she turned and walked away. He sat there for a moment, then very slowly peered around the side of the tombstone. The bogle walking away was extremely old and bent. She had her back to him, but as she melted into the mist, he could just make out the familiar wispy grey hair, fat belly and crooked walking stick.

It was indeed Belchetta Ballybog.

Granny crawled out from the bush, her hat wonky and her hair over one eye.

"I have prickles in places a lady should never have prickles," she said, wriggling her large bottom and frowning. "Did you get a good look at her, Barnaby?"

"Yes, I did," he said. "You're right – it was Belchetta."

They stood for a moment in stunned silence.

"I can't believe it," said Barnaby at last.

"Part of me was hoping it wasn't true," said Granny. "But we both saw her with our own eyes.

"And did you hear what she said?" he asked.

Granny shook her head and continued pulling thorns out of various parts of her body.

"She said 'good riddance to bad rubbish'."

Granny stopped what she was doing and stared at him, her face glowing. He hadn't seen her look so mad since the day she had fought Belchetta in the cellar. She took a deep breath in, and let out the loudest, phlegmiest sneezy-burp-screech ever.

"A – A – A –Tishabllllleauuuuuug-gggggghhhhooooo!"

Barnaby fell to the ground and waited for the dust around him to settle before glancing up at his grandmother. She was dabbing her large red nose with the small appliqué handkerchief, but her face was still glinting dangerously.

"Which way did she go?" she asked, angrily.

He pointed in the direction the bogle had gone and then watched in dismay as Granny strode forward and disappeared into the grey fog.

# CHAPTER 30
## Still Pickled

"Wait for me," shouted Barnaby as he tore after his grandmother.

She was just leaving the Bogle Burial Ground behind as he caught her up.

"Hurry," she said. "Belchetta can't have got very far. It looks like she's heading back into the village."

The bog-smog cleared and the temperature rose as they approached the round mud houses. Barnaby felt sick at the thought of Granny battling Belchetta again.

"Don't do anything silly," he panted.

"Remember how dangerous Belchetta is."

"I've got a permanent reminder of that," she said, rubbing her silvery skin.

"Don't fight her again," he pleaded. "Maybe I misheard her, and she didn't say 'good riddance to bad rubbish'."

"Maybe you did," said Granny, striding forward, "and I don't intend to fight her again. But we have to follow her, Barnaby, because if we find Belchetta, then we find your mother."

Barnaby nodded slowly.

"I didn't think about that," he said. "How could I be so daft?"

Granny looked him up and down.

"You get it from your father,"

she sniffed. "The only problem is … I think I've lost her."

They stopped and looked around. The mud-ball houses were all around them now, with the narrow gravel paths snaking out in different directions.

"It's OK," said Barnaby. "I was in her house last year. I remember where she lives. It's just round the corner."

"You are a clever boy," beamed Granny. "You get it from your mother."

Barnaby led Granny up a cramped alleyway and on to a wider street with a large house set back from the rest. It was at least six mud balls big. There was nobody around.

"I remember this place," cried Granny. "Belchetta lived here with her mother – my Aunt Burpina – when we were children."

"And she was still living here last year," said Barnaby. "It's where she held Dad prisoner."

"Hmm," said Granny, sidling up to the house and ducking beneath a window. "Sounds like she developed a taste for kidnapping."

Very slowly she peeked inside. Barnaby pressed his back against the wall of the house and looked anxiously up and down the road.

"Be careful, Granny," he whispered. "What can you see?"

Granny said nothing, but continued to stare through the window.

"What is it?" he asked.

She remained silent.

"Granny! Talk to me," he said, prodding her fleshy arm.

She jumped slightly but still looked into the house, a bewildered expression on her face.

"What are you looking at?" cried Barnaby in frustration.

"Oh … um … I'm looking at … Belchetta Ballybog," she said.

Barnaby's heart skipped a beat.

"Get down," he whispered. "She'll see you."

"I don't think that's possible," said Granny. "Take a look for yourself."

Barnaby slowly peeped over the window sill and peered into the large spherical chamber. His gaze travelled around the room, taking in the round table covered with a thick purple cloth embroidered with gold and the three bronze shields that hung on the walls, eventually coming to rest on a huge vat of vinegar with a pickled Belchetta still perfectly preserved inside.

# CHAPTER 31
## Stuck Again

Barnaby and Granny couldn't stop staring through the window at the pickled Belchetta.

"But that's impossible. We saw her at the Bogle Burial Ground," whispered Barnaby.

Granny got out her hankie and blew her nose, which was now as red as her lipstick.

"Anything is possible," she sniffed. "Oh, this stupid cold. A – A – Atishooooo!"

As the enormous sneeze rattled against the round house, a gnarled old bogle head popped up in front of them on the other side of the window. Barnaby recognized him immediately.

It was Ptolemy's uncle.

"Who's there?" he cried.

"Quick!" yelled Granny, pulling on Barnaby's arm. "Hide!"

They slipped behind the house and pressed themselves against a mud wall. They could hear the old bogle yelling inside.

"HUMANS!" he bellowed. "LOOKING INTO OUR HOUSE!"

"That's Ptolemy's uncle," panted Barnaby. "Apparently we're related. Do you know him?"

"He did look very familiar," whispered Granny. "But he is so old and wrinkled, and I only got a quick glimpse of him."

"HURRY!" shouted Ptolemy's uncle from inside. "BURPINA, COME QUICKLY."

Granny's face turned white.

"Burpina?" she gasped. "My Aunt Burpina is still alive? She must be a hundred years old."

"Dad said that there were other bogles living with Belchetta," said Barnaby. "Remember?"

"Yes, but I never thought for a moment that one of them would be her mother," said Granny, looking frantically around. "I thought she died years ago. We have to get out of here fast. Which way to the ladder?"

"But what about Mum?" cried Barnaby. "We can't just leave her here."

"I know, but we have to re-think," said Granny, pulling Barnaby down a gravel path. "Burpina Ballybog is the one who banished me."

"I'm not going to leave without my mum," he said, stopping in the middle of the path.

"I don't want to go without her either, you silly boy," said Granny, looking nervously behind him. "But returning back to Bogle Bog after being banished is punishable by toe-knuckle potion. Burpina could wipe our memories and then we would never be able to rescue your mum. She is a very powerful and dangerous bogle. You thought Belchetta was bad? You haven't met her mother."

Barnaby looked over his shoulder just in time to see two ancient bogles appear around the corner.

"It looks like I'm just about to," he said.

Burpina was the spitting image of her daughter. Her thin grey hair sprang out in random patches over her knobbly, domed head. Two glinting black eyes were almost hidden beneath folds of wrinkled liver-spotted skin. She was almost bent double, and the spiky grey whiskers on her chin pricked the top of her enormous belly.

They both waved crooked walking sticks which they didn't appear to need as they strode forward.

"There they are," she screeched, pointing her stick at them.

"We have to get to the ladder," said Granny.

Barnaby nodded, and they ran to the base of the enormous ladder. Granny went up first with Barnaby close behind.

"The situation is worse than I thought," she puffed, climbing higher and higher. "We're going to need some of my dark pickles. We have to get back to the cellar, and I'll see what I can rustle up."

They were almost at the top. Barnaby looked down below them. He could just make out the two old bogles slowly but surely climbing the ladder. Granny had reached the roots of the hollow tree and was hauling herself up.

"Quick," shouted Barnaby. "They're following us."

"I'm going as quickly as I can," she yelled. "But when you pulled me out of the tree last time, you dislodged some earth and it's blocking the way. I'm going to have to try and squeeze through."

He looked down nervously. Now he could clearly see the top of Ptolemy's uncle's head, closely followed by Burpina.

"Hurry," he called. "They're getting closer."

Granny had managed to squash her top half through the hollow tree.

"You are going to have to give me a push," she cried, her voice echoing from inside.

Barnaby looked up at Granny's bottom half and then down at the ascending bogles. He gritted his teeth and positioned himself directly beneath her, so that she was sitting on his shoulder like a huge, grotesque parrot. He clung to the ladder and pushed with all his might, but she didn't budge. He repositioned himself and tried to push at a different angle.

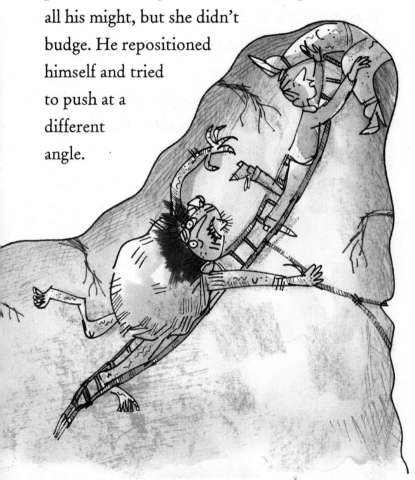

Her large bottom was enveloping his head like a huge beanbag. Just when he thought it couldn't get any worse, a large and bony hand wrapped itself around his ankle.

"Got him," croaked the old bogle.

"Well done, Baldric," screeched Burpina, beneath him. "You're a true Ballybog."

"Baldric Ballybog?" repeated Barnaby. He vaguely remembered Ptolemy saying that his uncle was called Baldric.

"Baldric Ballybog?" came Granny's muffled voice from above. "Father? Is that you?"

# CHAPTER 32

# The Toe-Knuckle Potion

Barnaby stared down at the bony old bogle whose large hand was still firmly wrapped around his ankle. This was Granny's dad?

"Father?" shouted Granny. "I thought you were dead. It's me – Beatrix."

"I'm not your father," he croaked. "What are you talking about? Now come down quietly or I'll pull the boy off the ladder."

He gave Barnaby's leg a hard tug.

"That's my grandson," yelled Granny. "Your great-grandson."

Barnaby clung to the ladder. He couldn't

take his eyes off his bogle great-grandfather. He was so wrinkled that it was hard to see any of his features and his spiky grey hair surrounded his face in a complete circle. But he was strong despite his age and held on to Barnaby's ankle in a vice-like grip.

"Why are you saying that?" he shouted. "You're just a … a … filthy human!"

Barnaby could feel the hand around his ankle begin to shake.

"Calm down, Baldric," shouted Burpina from below. "They are just trying to confuse you, dear brother. Let go of the boy, climb around me to the bottom of the ladder and fetch my personal bodyguards. It looks like the fleshy one is stuck in the tree."

"How dare you!" bellowed Granny, her loud voice echoing around the tree. "I am not fleshy. I am well-covered, and Baldric Ballybog is my father."

Baldric let go of Barnaby's leg and managed to climb around Burpina. Barnaby couldn't believe how agile they were.

"I'm not listening to any more of your rubbish," Baldric called, slowly clambering down.

Burpina waited until he was out of earshot.

"So, Beatrix Hogsflesh has returned, after all these years," she shouted up to Granny.

"It's pronounced *Ho-flay*, actually," said Granny in a loud voice. "And many years ago, you told me my father was dead."

"Well, he's dead as far as you're concerned,"

said Burpina. "Your father doesn't remember you any more. I erased part of his memory with my toe-knuckle potion."

Barnaby heard a loud gasp from inside the tree.

"But why?" shouted Granny.

"Because I wanted him to forget all about you and your horrible human mother. I hated your mother – that wretched Mary Morley," shrieked Burpina. "She took everything away from me. First my baby…"

"That was a misunderstanding," said Granny. "You got your baby back."

"Then she took my brother, Baldric, away from me," fumed Burpina. She was so angry that foam was spraying from her mouth. "She tricked him into marrying her by making him eat from the same beetroot as her, so they would fall in love."

"But she had to do that," said Barnaby, "to break the curse that *you* put on her."

"Silence, you horrid little human," screeched Burpina. "I'm not talking to you, I am talking to the fleshy one."

"I am positively svelte compared with you, madam," shrieked Granny.

"Anyway, I decided to reverse her little beet-root trick," continued Burpina, "by modifying their memories with my toe-knuckle potion. The plan was to send you and your mother back to the human world and leave Baldric here with me. But *poor* Mary Morley, being human, couldn't take the full dose and died ... oops!"

She laughed horribly. Barnaby looked up towards Granny. He could see her feet twitching.

"You killed her!" cried Granny.

"Yes, I suppose I did," said Burpina, still chuckling to herself. "Oh well!"

"Why didn't you give me any toe-knuckle potion?" asked Granny.

"I knew I wouldn't have to. You were so desperate to leave this place and live with the humans," said Burpina. "Anyone who drinks large amounts of toe-knuckle potion has similar symptoms to marsh fever – glazed eyes and memory loss. So I told you your parents had died from marsh fever and you never returned. Fine daughter you are."

"You banished me," cried Granny. "I couldn't return, even if I wanted to."

"But you didn't want to. You made it easy for me. My life was perfect again – you and your horrible mother were gone for ever and Baldric had no memory of you. But now you're back. You defied your banishment and returned."

"I suppose you intend to give me the toe-knuckle potion as punishment," said Granny.

"Not at all," croaked Burpina, anger lighting up her black eyes. "You committed a crime far worse than coming back to Bogle Bog. You pickled my daughter, and I have other plans for you."

"It was self-defence," shouted Granny. "She tried to kill us all."

"My little Belchetta wouldn't have harmed a fly," said Burpina.

Barnaby nearly fell off the ladder. Belchetta had tied them up, poisoned them with a burp from the Indo-Chinese Warty Pig, and stabbed Granny with a lethal pickled toenail.

"She just wanted what was rightfully hers – the Hogsflesh Pickle Company."

"*Ho-flay* Pickles," said Granny, haughtily, "belongs to me. What right has she to my factory?"

"You set up that factory with the money you

made from the dark side – the dark pickles," said Burpina. "And you stole those dark recipes from me."

Barnaby looked up, waiting to hear Granny's comeback. But there was silence.

# CHAPTER 33

# A Daughter for a Daughter

Burpina turned her attention to Barnaby.

"If you want to see your mother again, you beastly little human," she said, "then you had better come with me."

"So you're the kidnapper," said Barnaby. "You are BB – Burpina Ballybog."

"That's right," snarled Burpina. "She took my daughter –" she stabbed a long gnarled finger up at Granny – "so I took *her* daughter."

Barnaby looked up at Granny. She was well and truly wedged inside the hollow tree, blocking all means of escape.

"I'm sorry, Barnaby," she called down. "You will have to go with her; we have no choice."

He looked down at the ground and saw a small crowd gathering at the bottom. Burpina followed his gaze.

"Those are my personal bodyguards," she said. "The B-Team – an elite group of fighting bogles. So don't bother trying to escape."

"B-Team?" repeated Barnaby.

"They are my loyal followers," said Burpina, proudly. "As Bogle Chieftain, I like to keep them close."

"You're their leader?" gasped Barnaby.

"Of course I am," she barked. "Didn't your grandmother tell you anything? The Ballybogs are the ancestral chieftains of Bogle Bog."

Barnaby clung to the ladder in stunned silence. They were related to bogle royalty.

"It's going to take a lot of bogle power to pull

her out," Burpina said, gesturing up towards Granny. "I have a good mind to leave her there, but unfortunately she's blocking the exits and causing a fire hazard. So start moving, and no more questions."

She slowly began the long descent and Barnaby reluctantly followed.

"Barnaby," called Granny from above. "Catch."

Barnaby looked up to see a small jar falling from the hollow tree. He reached up and caught it just in time. He hurriedly read the label before slipping it into his pocket – *Selected Worm Burps.*

"I've got it, Granny," he said. "And don't worry; they have assembled a special team to pull you out."

"Oh, the humiliation!" cried Granny. "Hauled out of a tree by a bogle SWAT team."

Barnaby continued climbing down. His legs were shaking as he reached the ground. Burpina

and Baldric were waiting for him, surrounded by a group of the biggest, hairiest, ugliest bogles Barnaby had ever seen.

"What's that up there?" grunted one of them, pointing up the ladder towards Granny's dangling legs.

"My loyal followers," shouted Burpina, "that thing up there, stuck in the hollow tree, is Beatrix Hogsflesh – a traitor to the bogle race, and guilty of pickling my daughter, Belchetta."

There was a collective gasp, and

some of the bodyguards began shouting angrily. More bogles were approaching from all directions, eager to know what the commotion was. Barnaby's legs were shaking so much he almost fell over, but Baldric and Burpina grabbed hold of an arm each.

"Where is Musty?" shouted Burpina.

A bogle Barnaby recognized stepped forward. It was the same one that had pushed Ptolemy over when they first arrived in Bogle Bog.

"Take the other members of the B-Team," commanded Burpina, "climb up the ladder, pull her out and bring her to me."

A small crowd of bogles looked on as eight beefy members of the B-Team stormed up the ladder after Musty. Right at the back of the crowd, and standing motionless, Barnaby spotted a shocked-looking Ptolemy.

"Ptolemy!" shouted Barnaby. "Ptolemy!"

But the little bogle just bowed his head and stared at the ground.

"Silence," yelled Burpina, dragging Barnaby away from the crowd and through the streets towards her house.

"Ptolemy? He's my nephew," said Baldric, a confused expression on his face. "How do you know him?"

"Because he's my cousin," said Barnaby, "and you are my great-grandfather."

"Shut up, you little liar," snapped Burpina. "Don't listen to him, Baldric, he's trying to confuse and upset you. Remember – never trust a human."

Baldric's brow furrowed deeper.

"But you said the fleshy one was a traitor to the bogle race," he mumbled. "What does that mean?"

Burpina stopped abruptly; her face was red and frazzled.

"I think it's time for your medicine, dear brother," she said, pulling a tiny glass vial from her muddy dress. "Drink it all up now."

Baldric took the small bottle in his hand and gulped it down. The minute he did, the frown between his bushy eyebrows disappeared and his eyes glazed over.

"Where are we?" he asked, his jaw sagging open slightly.

"We are just taking this horrible little human to be with his mother," said Burpina, pulling Barnaby on. "They are guilty of pickling Belchetta."

"OK," he murmured quietly. They had reached the house.

"You go to your room and have a little nap," she said to him. "I will take care of the boy."

Baldric nodded vaguely and disappeared inside. Barnaby turned to Burpina.

"That was toe-knuckle potion, wasn't it?" he said. "You're still giving it to him, to keep his memory from returning."

Burpina said nothing, but her face twisted in a horrible toothless grin.

# CHAPTER 34
## Sabotage

Burpina pushed Barnaby through the front door into the round house. It was deceptively large inside. Three tunnels led off to different parts of the house. But it was the large vat filled with a pickled Belchetta that Barnaby was staring at.

"It was extremely difficult getting her here," said Burpina, looking into the vat. "Especially with your mother in tow. But my elite B-Team helped me, and with a bit of bogle know-how, we managed."

"If they're so elite, why are they called the *B-Team*?" asked Barnaby. "Shouldn't it be *A*?"

"B for bogle, you stupid boy," said Burpina.

Barnaby said nothing. He was thinking about the last time he had been in this house, when Belchetta had imprisoned his dad. Burpina seemed to read his thoughts and pushed him through one of the tunnels leading to a small room at the back of the house.

"You will be staying in the same room as your dear father did, when he was a guest here," she said.

"He wasn't your guest," said Barnaby. "You held him here against his will."

"Actually, that was Belchetta's idea," said Burpina. "She had this marvellous plan to take over Hogsflesh Pickles."

"*Ho-flay*," mumbled Barnaby.

"Obviously that plan failed," she said, ignoring him. "And when I found out what happened to my daughter, I decided to avenge her death, and carry on with her dream to secure the Hogsflesh Pickle Company for the Ballybogs."

"You don't know the first thing about the factory," said Barnaby.

"Oh yes I do," cackled Burpina. "Your security needs to be tightened up. I've managed to get in a few times and have a good look around. I left a couple of little surprises for you and your grandmother. One in the nuclear department…"

Barnaby gasped. "It was you who caused the explosion!"

"Yes," smiled Burpina. "It was supposed to be for you, but some silly scientist got in the way. And another little eye opener in the Vinaigrette – or should I say eye squasher."

"You sabotaged the airbag!" cried Barnaby.

"Hmm," said Burpina, stroking the thick whiskers on her chin. "That one was supposed to be for your grandmother. Still, as long as I got one of you…"

And with that, she opened a door and pushed him in, slamming and bolting it behind.

A loud hiccup from the other side of the room made Barnaby jump.

"BARNABY!"

Two arms grabbed him in a vice-like grip. He struggled for a moment, then looked up at the familiar face above him and relaxed into the comfort of his mum's hug.

"Barnaby, what are you doing here?" she said.

He put his head on her shoulder and hugged her back, relieved that she was all right.

"I've come to rescue you," he said. "Are you OK? What happened?"

"Yes, I'm fine," she said. "I was working in the cellar when the intruder alarm went off. I turned and there must have been at least ten bogles standing there, with Burpina in front. I was terrified. For a moment, I thought it was Belchetta."

"I know," said Barnaby. "They're almost identical."

"And not just in looks," said Mum. "Burpina jumped on me and held a stinky cloth against my nose and mouth. I passed out with the fumes and woke up here. She told me I was being held for ransom."

"Yes, she wants the factory," said Barnaby.

"But you've come to rescue me," said Mum, squeezing him again. "So, what's the plan?"

Barnaby took a step back and sat down on the bed in the middle of the room.

"Plan?" he asked.

Mum's eyes narrowed and she sat down slowly beside him.

"Yes, plan," she said, "to get out of here."

Barnaby stared down at his feet.

"There is no plan, is there?" she sighed. "Now we're both in danger. Where are Dad and Granny? Do they know you're here?"

"Granny's here too," he said. "She's causing congestion problems and fire hazards."

"She's doing what?"

At that moment the door flew open and Granny marched in, her face shining menacingly.

"…and if you ever try and touch my feather again, you impudent worm," she yelled, "I will karate chop your *other* hand."

Musty and the rest of the B-Team were crowding round the door. They all looked completely bedraggled and extremely stunned. Musty was holding his hand and wincing.

"She's scary," he grunted, turning to go.

The others followed, looking warily at Granny as the door banged shut and the bolt slammed into place.

"Hatty!" cried Granny. "Are you all right?"

"I'm fine," said Mum. "What about you?"

"Not too bad, apart from a bit of a cold."

"Not just any old cold," said Barnaby. "It's a rhino cold."

"I'm fine," said Granny, blowing her nose.

"Stop fussing."

"What happened with that lot?" asked Barnaby, pointing at the closed door.

"Burpina's hench-bogles pulled me out of that awful tree," sniffed Granny. "I hate that tree! And then they had the audacity to herd me through the streets like some sort of large bovine beast."

Barnaby looked questioningly at his mum.

"Like a cow," she explained.

"Exactly," said Granny.

"They needed to be taught some manners. So I gave one of them a kizami tsuki to the nose."

"A kizami what?"

"It's a karate punch," she said, demonstrating, "more of a jab, really."

"I didn't know you still did karate, Mother," said Mum.

"Yes, dear, Monday nights after choir practice," she said. "I then stunned the lot of them with a pickled turkey trump, before delivering a sweeping butterfly twist..."

She jumped high in the air, swinging her legs round in an armless cartwheel.

"... knocking two of them completely off the path."

Barnaby's jaw dropped open.

"Hopefully they'll think twice before attacking a defenceless old lady again."

"Not that defenceless," murmured Mum.

The sound of the bolt on the door being drawn back made them all turn as Burpina marched in. She smiled threateningly at them all, and put some papers on a side table with a pen on top.

"I took the liberty of drawing up some legal documents," she said, "transferring the Hogsflesh Pickle Company over to my control. You just need to sign them."

"NEVER!" yelled Granny.

Burpina continued smiling.

"You have until tomorrow morning to reconsider," she said. "Or your daughter and grandson will face a public pickling."

# CHAPTER 35
# Beetroot Memories

Burpina left the room, slamming the door behind her. Barnaby looked up at his mum, his eyes wide, and sat down on the bed. She followed and put her arm around him.

"It's a bluff," said Granny, pacing the small room. "Burpina wouldn't pickle you – she couldn't. She doesn't have the know-how. Nobody understands the delicate complexity of the dark pickling fluids like me. It's not just vinegar, you know."

"She's managed to keep Belchetta preserved," said Mum.

"Not for long," said Granny. "The temperature's all wrong, the lighting's all wrong, and she hasn't put the right ingredients into the vinegar. I could smell it as I walked past, despite this terrible cold. I happen to be blessed with a prodigious pickling nose."

Barnaby would have laughed if he wasn't feeling so terrified.

"You can't be sure what she's capable of," he said. "You said yourself that she was your inspiration for turning to the dark side."

Granny sneezed loudly and continued walking around the small room, her eyebrows pulled into a deep frown.

"Inspiration – maybe," she said. "But to say that I stole her recipes is ridiculous. She has no right to my factory."

"So what are we going to do?" asked Mum.

Granny stopped pacing and sat down heavily

beside them, making Barnaby bounce up.

"When I was stuck in that stupid tree for the second time," she said, "your little dog, Morley, was still waiting patiently at the top. I sent him for help. I told him to go and fetch your father. Whether a dumb animal will understand is another thing."

"Oh, he'll understand," cried Barnaby. "I bet he's tugging on Dad's sleeve right now."

"That's all well and good," said Mum, getting up and pulling at the bolted door. "But we can't rely on Morley to save us."

To her surprise the door opened, and standing in the doorway was Baldric Ballybog, a tray of food in his arms.

"There's no point trying to escape," he said, coming in and placing the tray on a table. "The front door is locked, there is no back door, and Burpina is in the main room."

He turned to go.

"Wait, don't leave yet," said Granny. "Stay and talk for a minute. Tell me … um … what have you brought for us to eat?"

As Baldric looked down at the tray, Granny signalled to Mum to close the door behind him. But he looked up and saw her.

"Don't you go trying any of your nonsense," he said. His watery old eyes still seemed to be glazed over. "I might be old, but I'm still as strong as an ox."

"Same as me," said Granny. "But then again, I would be, wouldn't I … being your daughter."

Mum hiccuped loudly in surprise.

"That's your father?" she gasped.

Granny nodded as Baldric frowned and walked towards the door.

"I don't have a daughter," he said. "You are trying to confuse me. Burpina told me to be careful. Never trust a human, she said."

"Don't go yet," said Granny. "Please, tell me what these delicious-looking dishes are."

Barnaby peered down at the tray of food on the table. He hadn't eaten for hours and was starving. There were three small plates covered with short transparent worms, with dirt sprinkled on top. He was sure one of the wormy things was still moving.

"Poached beetle grubs, topped with tree bark shavings," said Baldric, proudly. "You might be our prisoners, but I believe you should still eat well."

Barnaby's appetite suddenly disappeared.

"How kind," said Granny, sitting at the table and pulling

a jar out of her pocket. "I find that beetroot goes terribly well with poached beetle grubs."

*What is she up to?* thought Barnaby.

"Beetroot?" repeated Baldric. He started to look confused again. "I think I once knew someone who ate beetroot."

"Really?" asked Granny, opening the lid and handing him the jar. "Have a little smell. See if it brings back any – memories."

Barnaby realized that Granny was trying to get him to remember her mother. Baldric's wife had been a beetroot farmer. It made her hands turn purple and she could never get rid of the smell.

"It does smell familiar," said Baldric, sniffing the beetroot. A small smile touched the sides of his hairy face. "It's a nice memory … very vague … very far away…"

Granny took her fork, hooked out a large sliver of beetroot and slapped it on top of the beetle grubs, turning them purple. "Beetroot and beetle grubs – yum."

She stabbed her fork into a large grub and a white pus seeped out. She mopped it up with a slice of beetroot and popped the whole thing into her mouth. Barnaby's stomach clenched involuntarily.

"Mmm, delicious!" she said, chewing slowly and deliberately. "Try some."

She pulled a second jar of beetroot from her pocket and pushed it towards Baldric. He slowly unscrewed the lid, picked up a fork and dipped it into the beetroot, pulling out a large slice. He smelled it again before stuffing it into his mouth. Some juice squirted out, giving his grey beard purple highlights. His face grew thoughtful as he chewed and Barnaby thought his glazed eyes began to look sharper.

"The taste, the smell..." he muttered, "it reminds me of a girl ... a woman."

"Yes," whispered Granny. "She was called Mary."

"Mary?" he murmured. "I dream about a Mary, but she's not real, she doesn't exist."

"She was real," said Granny, urgently. "She was your wife, my mother."

Barnaby and his mum held their breath as Granny went on.

"Have some more."

Baldric picked up the jar and was about to dip his fork in again when he stopped suddenly and glared at Granny, his black eyes narrowing to tiny slits.

"You're trying to trick me," he muttered. "You're confusing me again."

"No," cried Granny. "It's true."

"Get away from me," he yelled, storming towards the door. "You're nothing but lying, deceitful humans."

He hurled the jar of beetroot at Granny. She managed to duck out of the way and it smashed against the wall, spraying everyone with purple juice. Then he stomped out of the door, banging it firmly behind him.

# CHAPTER 36
# Night-time Excursions

Barnaby's mum gave everyone a tissue to wipe off the beetroot juice.

"So, your dad is still alive," she said to Granny. "That must have been a shock."

Granny just nodded and blew her nose loudly on the tissue Mum handed her.

"It was," said Barnaby. "And that's not all. We're related to bogle royalty. Burpina is their leader. She's the chief."

"Chief*tain*," corrected Granny, wiping her nose. "And it shouldn't be her. It should be my father. He's slightly older than her. He used to be the Bogle Chieftain."

"You never told us that," gasped Mum. "That makes you a bogle princess."

"It doesn't work like that," sniffed Granny. "Although I do have many royal qualities."

"So, how come he's not in charge any more?" asked Barnaby.

"It looks like Burpina took over when she erased his memory," said Granny. "We have to make him remember who he was and who I am. It could save us."

"That's what you were doing with the beetroot," said Mum. "Good try."

"I haven't finished yet," said Granny, looking down at the beetroot jar she was eating from. "I've said it before and I'll say it again – never underestimate the power of a beetroot. I have hidden the pickles I had in my bag in my clothes, in case of emergencies. And if I can just stop

Burpina from giving Baldric more toe-knuckle potion, I think I can get his memory to return."

"You were really brave, eating that horrible dinner," said Barnaby.

"What are you talking about?" said Granny. "Poached beetle grubs was my favourite dinner when I was growing up. And I suggest you tuck in too. Goodness knows when we'll eat again."

Barnaby pulled a face and sank down on to the bed. He suddenly felt exhausted. It felt like it had been one of the longest days of his life.

"She's right," said his mum. "I've eaten all sorts of grubs since I've been here, and you soon get used to them."

"Maybe later," he murmured. "First we must think of a way to escape before morning."

"I've tried once already," said Mum, "but the windows are too small for me to squeeze through. Any other ideas?"

Barnaby laid back on the bed and tried to think of an escape plan, but he couldn't seem to focus. He could hear Mum and Granny talking quietly, their voices floating around the room, and his eyes slowly closed.

When he opened them again, it was morning. Mum was fast asleep beside him, and Granny was snoring loudly in a chair.

"Wake up!" he cried. "We're getting pickled this morning!"

Mum stirred beside him.

"What time is it?" she asked.

"It's pickling time!" he shouted. "How could we have fallen asleep? Last night was our only chance of escaping."

Lots of loud burping and grunting noises started coming from Granny's chair.

"Where am I?" she croaked, sitting up.

"We're still in Burpina's house," said Barnaby, "when we should have been escaping."

"It's impossible," said Mum. "Your granny and I had a good look around last night after you went to sleep."

"Did you get out of the room?" he asked.

"Yes, Baldric left the door unlocked when he stormed out. We managed to have a look around the house, but like I said, all the windows are too small to get out of and the front door is locked. We thought we might be able to dig our way out, but Burpina found us and brought us back in here."

"Why didn't you kizami tsuki her, Granny?" asked Barnaby.

"Believe me, I wanted to," she said, "but I'm afraid the house is completely surrounded by the B-Team, and there are just too many of them, even for me."

"So we've failed," said Barnaby. "It's either sign the factory over, or be pickled."

"Not quite," said Granny. "Your mother found a cupboard full of toe-knuckle potion. We managed to empty the lot down the sink just before we were discovered. Burpina was furious."

"Sounds like I missed out on a busy night," he said.

"I think today will make up for that," said Mum, as the bolts of the door slammed across and it creaked open.

Burpina stood in the doorway, Baldric just behind her.

"Tired out after our night-time excursions, are we?" she sneered.

Mum and Granny just glared at her as she strode in and picked up the legal documents she had left with them yesterday.

"Have you signed Hogsflesh Pickles over to

me yet?" she demanded.

"Certainly not," said Granny. "You can't even pronounce it properly, let alone run it."

Burpina smiled and slowly walked towards Granny, not stopping until their noses were almost touching.

"Then prepare to see your loved ones pickled!" she rasped.

# CHAPTER 37
# To Sign or Not to Sign

Barnaby looked nervously from Granny to his mum.

"I don't think she's bluffing," he said. "She wants to pickle us."

Burpina laughed uproariously. "Of course I want to pickle you," she said, "but I want that factory more."

"You wouldn't pickle them," said Granny. "You don't even know how to."

"Oh yes I do," said Burpina. "I took some of your pickling equipment back with me when I got Belchetta from your cellar."

"So you're a thief as well as a kidnapper," shouted Granny.

"Would you like them back after I've pickled your family?" asked Burpina. "The B-Team have constructed a large wooden stage in the middle of the Landing Square, with two big vats of vinegar in the middle. We want to make sure that everyone can see." She handed a pen and the legal documents over to Granny. "So, it's either sign the factory over to me, or sit back and watch the public pickling."

"The dark side of pickling is an intricate and complex business," sneered Granny, pushing away the pen. "It's too much for your small bogle brain to cope with."

"Don't underestimate me," hissed Burpina, reaching towards Barnaby. "I know exactly how to pickle them – just watch me."

"Get your bony hands off my grandson,"

yelled Granny, rearing up like a praying mantis about to strike.

There was a loud crash as Musty came storming through the door, closely followed by eight more members of the B-Team.

"I wouldn't do anything stupid if I were you," said Burpina, holding her hands up defensively. "As well as the B-Team, the bogles outnumber you a hundred to one, and if anything happens to me, then your family will never leave the bog."

Granny hesitated, then slowly sat down at the table.

"Give me the pen," she said, angrily.

Barnaby watched as Burpina triumphantly handed it over.

"Wait!" cried Mum. "You love that factory. It's your life's work. It means everything to you."

Granny looked up at Mum and Barnaby.

"Not everything," she said, quietly.

"STOP!" shouted Barnaby, as she began to sign. "Don't do it. We still have time. Morley will get help, I know it."

Granny hesitated.

"SIGN IT!" shrieked Burpina.

"No!" yelled Mum. "Barnaby's right. We still have time."

Granny nodded slowly, then put the pen down, and looked defiantly up at the furious Burpina.

"So, you have made your choice," she snapped. "Musty, show our guests the way out."

Musty pushed past Baldric, who was watching the events silently from the doorway, a worried look on his face.

"Come along, dear brother," said Burpina. "We have a very special event to attend."

"But, sister," he said, "I'm not feeling well. You haven't given me my medicine this morning."

Burpina glared at Mum and Granny. "I'm afraid these shifty she-devils destroyed your medicine," she said, angrily. "You will have to wait until I can make some more."

"But I get confused without it," he said. "I start having strange thoughts and dreams."

"They're not dreams," cried Granny as she was jostled out the door by the B-Team. "They are memories; they're real. Your medicine is actually toe-knuckle potion. Burpina is feeding tiny amounts to you so you can never remember your family."

"SILENCE!" yelled Burpina. "*I* am your family, Baldric. Stop listening to these lies. These people pickled Belchetta and now they are going to pay the price."

The frown on Baldric's forehead deepened as he followed everyone out of the bedroom and along the corridor to the main spherical room.

Musty stood by the front door, with the rest of the B-Team lining the round walls. Barnaby glanced nervously at the big glass vat with the pickled Belchetta inside. He was sure that she wasn't as well-preserved as the last time he had looked. Her hair had completely disintegrated. Maybe Granny was right and Burpina didn't know how to pickle things.

Musty flung the door open and pushed Barnaby, Mum and Granny out in front of him, where a small crowd of bogles were waiting for them.

"We've brought reinforcements," said Musty, looking warily at Granny.

"Take them to the Landing Square," ordered Burpina. "It's time for revenge – revenge of the Ballybogs!"

# CHAPTER 38
# The Raspberry Mega-horn

"REVENGE OF THE BALLYBOGS!" shouted the B-Team. "REVENGE OF THE BALLYBOGS!"

The chanting bogles pushed Barnaby, Mum and Granny down a narrow muddy path.

"REVENGE OF THE BALLYBOGS!" The crowd began to join in. "REVENGE OF THE BALLYBOGS!"

"How long must we endure this?" whispered Granny to Barnaby. "We're running out of time, and we can't rely on a dog to save us."

"Morley will do it," said Barnaby, looking all

around him. "He'll fetch Dad."

"If that's our only hope, then we're doomed," hissed Granny. "We have to fight back soon."

"Not yet," said Barnaby. "You stick close to Baldric and try to get his memory back. If he remembers you, then he could stop this whole thing happening."

"OK," she murmured, striding forward to walk beside Baldric. Barnaby looked around for his mum, but she had been jostled to the back of the crowd. He could see Burpina elbowing her way towards him.

"What were you two whispering about?" she said, barging her way through. "Keep on moving."

She pushed him roughly in the back.

Barnaby stumbled on a rock and fell face down in the foul boggy ground. Two large knobbly hands clamped around his shoulders, turned him over and hauled him to his feet. He looked up into the fierce black eyes of the most monstrous bogle he had ever seen.

The whole of the bogle's face was covered in prickly black hair. His long, crooked nose sprouted thick tufts of nostril whiskers, which waved menacingly in the air as he snorted in excitement. Barnaby's gaze travelled slowly down to the two big bottom teeth that poked out of the bogle's jutting jaw, almost reaching those terrible fluttering nostrils.

Barnaby staggered forward, frantically looking around for a way to escape. But he was completely surrounded. More bogles appeared from every direction. They were closing in, burping and grunting in anticipation, herding him along the dark, muddy road towards the main square.

A small crowd had gathered there, looking up at a large wooden stage. A high timber frame stood in the centre, with two big slings dangling ominously down. Under the slings was a pair of enormous jars. Barnaby could smell the vinegar before he reached them and his knees began to tremble.

The monstrous bogle pushed him up some rough steps on to the stage. Granny was already there, standing next to Baldric. Mum followed with Burpina close behind. Burpina grabbed what looked like a huge megaphone. Barnaby realized it was actually a hollow tree root, shaped like a horn with spindly twigs still attached. She stuck out her thick purple tongue and moistened her big lips before taking an enormous breath. She pressed it to her mouth and blew the biggest raspberry he had ever heard in his life. The little round houses shook with the vibration as the sound went on and on. Heads popped out of windows, doors opened and gradually crowds of noisy bogles came swarming into the square, pointing up at the stage. There was an air of excitement and confusion.

"What's going on?" cried one.

"It must be important," shouted another. "The raspberry mega-horn is only used in emergencies."

Eventually Burpina stopped blowing and held her hands up for quiet.

"Fellow bogles," she called. The noise died down. "As your leader, you know that I would never summon you with the raspberry mega-horn without a good reason."

There was more talking and murmuring as the bogles stared up at Barnaby and Mum, who were either side of Burpina. The B-Team flanked the stage, and Baldric was standing with Granny, holding her arm tightly. She was talking to him urgently. Barnaby noticed her press a jar of pickled beetroot into his other hand.

"I called you here today," continued Burpina, "to witness a public pickling."

There was a collective intake of breath, followed by a lot of noise.

"These filthy humans," shouted Burpina, above the racket, "pickled my only daughter, Belchetta."

Barnaby shrank back as scores of surprised and angry bogle faces burned into his.

"We all know the law," Burpina screeched. "An

eye for an eye, and a beard for a beard."

Mum pulled Barnaby behind her as the noise level increased.

"They pickled one of us, so I will pickle *two* of them," cried Burpina. "Strap them into the dunkers!"

"NO!" shouted Granny. But before she could do anything the B-Team immediately surrounded her.

Musty grabbed hold of Barnaby. Mum tried to pull him off, but she was pushed away by the bogle with the jutting bottom teeth and hairy nostrils.

"Let go of her, Tufty-Nose!" yelled Barnaby.

But he just snorted angrily. "My name is Hogarth," he grunted, pulling Mum towards the other sling.

"Wait!" cried a voice from the crowd.

Barnaby looked up to see Ptolemy stepping forward. He looked tiny beside the other bogles around him.

"How do we know they're guilty?" he shouted, as Mum and Barnaby were strapped into the giant slings. "We haven't heard their side of the story."

"The evidence is in my house," continued Burpina. "The B-Team have all seen the terrible fate of my daughter."

There were more gasps and grunts as members of the B-Team nodded solemnly.

"It was self-defence," shouted Granny. "Belchetta was trying to kill us."

"Silence!" yelled Burpina. "We cannot trust the testimony of deceitful humans."

Suddenly, the ground beneath Barnaby fell away as he was hoisted high above the huge vat of vinegar.

"STOP!" shouted Ptolemy from below. "They are not human – they have bogle blood running through their veins."

The crowd turned to Burpina.

"Ptolemy Tatty," she yelled, "mind your own business."

"It is my business," he shouted. "They are relatives."

"It's true!" bellowed Granny. "You may not recognize me. I left over fifty years ago. But my name was Beatrix Ballybog. I grew up here."

A ripple of excitement filtered through the crowd. Baldric's head shot up, and Burpina cleared her throat and smoothed down her muddy frock.

"As some of you may know," she said, her voice shaking slightly, "there was a family scandal many, many years ago. This did indeed lead to human blood contaminating the great

Ballybog name. It was agreed at the time never to be talked about, as my dear brother, Baldric, never fully recovered from the ordeal and has been left permanently dazed and confused."

Baldric's eyes narrowed when his name was mentioned. Granny reached across him and slowly unscrewed the lid of the beetroot he was holding, wafting the smell under his nose.

"So I will thank you, Ptolemy Tatty, never to mention it again." continued Burpina, "However, bearing their bogle ancestry in mind, I will agree not to pickle them if, and only if, they agree to hand over the Hogsflesh Pickle Company to bogle control."

There was a lot of noise from the crowd.

"We don't want a pickle factory," cried one.

"I don't even like pickles," said another.

"Be quiet, you fools," shouted Burpina. "Don't you see? The income from that factory would make us all rich and powerful. We could reveal ourselves to the human race and find new and better ways to torment them. They would be under our control. We could force them to live underground, hiding their very existence, like we have had to do for centuries."

The B-Team started cheering, but other bogles looked unsure.

"I like living underground. I love the bog," said Ptolemy. "So do most bogles."

"Of course we do," cried a ginger bogle with a fiery red beard. "We are the guardians of the bog. What do we want with a pickle factory?"

The B-Team stopped cheering as the feeling in the crowd began to shift.

"We don't want a factory, and we don't want to pickle anyone," shouted Ptolemy. "So release the prisoners!"

Burpina turned on him, her face bright purple with fury.

"If you say one more word, Ptolemy Tatty," she shrieked, "I will have you arrested for treason."

"But they're not guilty," shouted Ptolemy. "Let them go."

"Then who did it?" called one of the crowd. "Who pickled Belchetta?"

"I did," came a loud and familiar voice.

Barnaby looked down to see Granny addressing the crowd. She was next to Baldric, who was chewing on something, his grey beard splashed with purple beetroot juice.

"It was me who pickled Belchetta," she announced.

There was a stunned silence.

"These two are not guilty!" she cried, pointing up at Barnaby and Mum. "Belchetta Ballybog attacked us in our own home. She tried to kill us! I did it to protect my daughter and grandson. I know that family loyalty is extremely important to bogles, and so I ask you to understand, and to set these innocent people free."

The crowd began shouting and arguing again.

"I've had enough of this," yelled Burpina. "I don't care if they did it or not. Are you going to sign over that factory to me or not?"

"Not!" cried Granny.

"Very well, you have made your choice," she screeched. "Lower the dunkers."

# CHAPTER 39
## Into the Vinegar

Barnaby's heart pounded wildly as Musty and Hogarth began turning a pair of enormous winch wheels. Wound around the wheels were the ropes that held Barnaby and his mum in the air. As the bogles turned the wheels, the dunkers were lowered towards the huge vats of pickling vinegar.

"No," cried Granny, breaking free from Baldric, "let them go."

"Grab her," cried Burpina to the B-Team. Granny tried to get away, but there were too many of them and she was eventually overcome.

"Lower her in first," shouted Burpina, pointing at Mum and grinning over at Granny. "A daughter for a daughter."

Barnaby wriggled against the straps that held him into the dunker as Hogarth slowly lowered Mum down. Barnaby's hand brushed against something hard in his pocket. It was the pickled worm burps.

"NO!" he yelled, pulling the small jar from his pocket. "She's done nothing wrong. Somebody help us – Ptolemy – Baldric – anyone!"

Mum had lifted her feet high in the air but was still heading towards the vinegar, bottom first.

A tiny figure shot out from the crowd and climbed on to the platform.

"Do something," yelled Ptolemy to the confused crowd. "They are innocent. Don't let this happen."

"Seize him!" shouted Burpina. "And any

others who defy me."

Mum's bottom was an inch away from the huge vat of vinegar as Musty left Barnaby's winch wheel and dragged Ptolemy away.

"Ptolemy, catch!" yelled Barnaby, flinging the worm burps down to him. The little bogle managed to grab the jar.

"Throw it at him," shouted Barnaby. "He will lose control of his muscles."

Ptolemy pulled out the stopper and threw the fizzing brown liquid into Musty's face, just as the tip of the sling dipped into the cold vinegar. Musty began to cough and splutter, and then twitch and jerk around the stage in a bizarre dance. But it was too late. Hogarth continued to lower the dunker, and the vinegar rippled as Mum touched the surface, making her hiccup in terror.

"AAAAA–hic–AAAAGGGH!"

"STOP!" bellowed Granny from beneath the B-Team. "Get her out! Wind her up! I'll sign the factory over to you. I'll sign anything!"

Burpina nodded to the winding bogle, and Mum was inched upwards. Barnaby heaved a sigh of relief as Musty jerked right off the stage and fell into the crowd.

"Mum, are you all right?" he called down.

"Yes," she said. "But I think I might have a pickled bottom."

Burpina marched triumphantly towards Granny and thrust the legal documents into her hands. Granny looked up at Barnaby and Mum swinging above the two vats.

"I have to do it," she said. "We've run out of time."

She took the pen and held it against the paper, hesitating for a moment as a strange howling sound drifted out of one of the holes high on the rock face by the side of the square. The howling got louder and everyone turned to see where it was coming from.

"Sign it," screeched Burpina. "Sign it now or else I'll—"

But before she could finish, Morley came flying out of one of the holes in the rock face, landing on a soft bed of moss. He was yowling and barking at the same time.

"WHISKER-FINK!" yelled someone. The crowd started to panic. Terrified screams filled the square as bogles ran in all directions. Morley charged through them, barking excitedly as he spotted Barnaby high up in the dunker. He leapt up on to the wooden platform, knocking several members of the B-Team off the stage, and Granny clean off her feet. The document she was about to sign fell into the panicking crowd and was trampled underfoot.

"NOOOOOOO!" Burpina screamed. "You planned this."

She jumped on top of Granny and wrapped her bony hands around her shoulders, shaking her angrily.

"I did not!" shouted Granny, karate chopping her hands away and flipping Burpina over on to her back.

"PICKLE THE WOMAN," screeched Burpina, as Granny sat on top of her. "PICKLE THE DAUGHTER – NOW!"

Granny turned towards Hogarth, her face distraught as he spun the winch round. Barnaby screamed and looked on helplessly as his mother splashed down into the large pickling vat.

# CHAPTER 40
# Mum's Last Stand

The moment Barnaby's mum hit the vinegar, a large human bullet came shooting out of another hole in the rock face. It flew across the crowd of panicking bogles, feet first, red hair flying out behind.

"DAD!" shouted Barnaby, as his father crash landed into the pickling vat, smashing it to pieces. Fergus Figg lifted his wife out of the shattered jar. Barnaby was relieved to see she could walk, but they were both covered in cuts.

"I'm coming back for you, Barnaby," Dad shouted, pulling Mum off the wooden stage.

Granny was still sitting on top of Burpina, with Morley beside her, barking.

"Well done, Fergus!" she cried. It was the first nice thing Barnaby had ever heard her say to him. "Is she OK?"

"A few cuts, and suffering from shock," said Dad, sitting Mum on the ground and wrapping his jacket around her, "but thankfully not pickled."

"She wasn't in there long enough for any lasting effects," said Granny. "I'll keep Burpina under control while you get Barnaby down."

Burpina struggled furiously beneath Granny.

"You can't control me," she screamed, as several large pairs of hands grabbed Granny from behind and pulled her off. She turned to see Baldric, helped by members of the B-Team.

"Thank you, dear brother," she said, staggering to her feet. "I feel like I've been sat on by a purple hippo."

Granny gasped in fury and lashed out at the big bogles.

"Make sure she can't get away," shouted Burpina, "and get these two."

She pointed over at Mum and Dad, who were immediately grabbed by a still-jiggling Musty and the rest of the B-Team. Morley snapped around Burpina's heels, barking and growling. She bent down and picked him up by the scruff of his neck, holding him close to her face. He stopped yapping as her small black eyes bored into his big brown ones. The panicking crowd below seemed to calm down as Morley fell silent and was lifted high into the air.

"Whisker-finks don't scare me," she croaked. "Someone fetch me a sack."

Barnaby watched in alarm as a particularly large bogle shot off and returned a minute later with a big bag. Burpina stuffed a surprised

Morley into the sack and handed him back to the wary bogle. She then turned to Dad.

"You have broken one of my pickling jars," she said, glancing round at the shattered glass, "but I still have one left." She looked up to where Barnaby was dangling over the vat. "These bogles have gathered to see a public pickling, and I don't want to let them down."

Barnaby's hands and feet suddenly went numb as he realized he was next. Dad began to struggle against the bogles holding him down as Mum slowly got to her feet. She looked up at Barnaby and her eyes seemed to glow as they locked with his. He had seen that look before, and almost felt sorry for the bogles standing either side of her.

She was one of the gentlest people he knew, but when she got angry, she was ferocious.

"Let my son go," Mum said in a loud, clear voice.

Burpina started cackling.

"I hardly think you are in a position to be making demands," she crowed.

Quick as a flash, Mum yanked the beards of her two restraining bogles, then leapt in one bound on to the stage. She grabbed Hogarth, who was standing by the winch, flipped him over and dangled him upside down by his ankles.

"What a woman!" cried Dad from beneath the small pile of bogles.

"That's my girl," yelled Granny, breaking away from the B-Team that surrounded her. She pulled something from an inside pocket and threw it to Mum, before being held firmly again. "Here, catch!"

Mum caught the small jar with one hand while

still holding the struggling bogle with the other. A nervous hush descended on the crowd as they waited to see what was going to happen. Mum looked at the jar and then at Granny.

"I thought we had run out of dark pickles," she said, holding it up.

"We have," said Granny. "That's from our skin and beauty department – pickled hair removal cream."

"Even better," said Mum, fiercely.

"PUT ME DOWN!" screamed Hogarth. "All the blood is rushing to my whiskers."

Mum held him up higher.

"Let my son go," she said again, "or I'll dissolve his beard!"

# CHAPTER 41
## Dissolving Whiskers

Hogarth gasped in terror as the horrified crowd turned to Burpina.

"You wouldn't dare dissolve his beard," she said.

"Oh yes I would," said Mum, unscrewing the jar with one hand.

"Nooooooo!" he screamed. "Please ... I have a wife and children."

Burpina stared at him, a horrible sneer touching the corners of her wide mouth.

"Go on, then," she said. "Do it. He means nothing to me."

The crowd gulped and burped in disbelief. Some stared at Burpina in stunned silence. Mum looked down at the shaking bogle she was holding.

"I'm begging you," he pleaded. "A bogle's beard means everything."

She hesitated and a look of concern crossed her face. She began to lower him down on to the ground.

"I don't want to," she began, "but I need help … my son…"

Barnaby noticed Burpina was slowly reaching for a small rock on the ground.

"Mum, watch out," he shouted.

But the rock was already hurtling through the air. As it struck her on the temple she fell to the ground, Hogarth landing in a heap beside her.

"Hatty!" shouted Granny, but the crumpled figure didn't move.

Hogarth staggered on to his knees. "She wasn't going to do it," he murmured, checking Mum. "You've knocked her out."

"Good," screeched Burpina. "Back to the winch, Hogarth. We have wasted enough time."

"But she wasn't going to dissolve my whiskers," he said. "I saw it in her eyes."

"Get back to the winch," she yelled.

But Hogarth ignored her and began walking away. "After everything that I did to her," he muttered quietly, "she wasn't going to do it. I thought humans were supposed to be evil."

"They are evil," screamed Burpina. "Hogarth! Where are you going? Get back here right now!"

But Hogarth had disappeared into the shocked crowd.

Burpina looked furious.

"Musty," she called. "Take up Hogarth's position. Let the dunking commence."

Musty hesitated for a moment. He looked out at the anxious bogles. Many had crowded round Hogarth, making sure he was all right.

"Move it!" yelled Burpina.

Musty jerked over to the big wheel attached to the dunker. Granny turned to Baldric, who was still holding her firmly. They were completely surrounded by members of the B-Team.

"Don't let this happen," she pleaded. "He is your great-grandson…"

Baldric's grip tightened.

"… and I am your daughter, Beatrix. You must remember. You taught me how to gather caterpillar cocoons, how to make mud pies. I could belch louder and harder than anyone else – you were so proud."

Baldric frowned and opened his mouth to speak but Burpina's voice drowned him out.

"Proceed with the pickling," she commanded.

Barnaby's heart hammered against his chest as he was jerked down, centimetre by centimetre, towards the murky brown vinegar. As he tried to hoist himself up the rope with his hands, he heard a fierce cry, and looked over to see Granny spinning round on one leg, knocking the B-Team flying with the other, and Dad pulling against the four bulky bogles holding him down.

"Hang in there, Barnaby," called his dad. "Help is on its way."

Barnaby lifted his legs high in the air, just as he had seen his mum doing.

"I need help right now," he shouted, as the stench of vinegar engulfed him.

Granny had despatched the B-Team and was now grappling with her own father.

"I didn't come here on my own," yelled Dad, still struggling with the bogles holding him fast. "Just hang on. They will be here any minute now."

"Who?" cried Barnaby.

Just as he was about to enter the jar, Barnaby saw five figures explode through the holes in the rock, landing randomly into the crowd.

"Hold it right there!" cried one in a loud, breathy voice, staggering to her feet.

"Nobody move a muscle," boomed another, pushing her way through the crush of confused bogles.

The winch stopped suddenly, leaving Barnaby dangling just above the vat. He peered through the haze of vinegar fumes to see a wiry grey head climb on to the platform. As she approached, the acrid smell of vinegar was mixed with something else, something spicier – meatballs.

"Mrs Wolfgruber?" he gasped.

"It's the Ladies' Pickled Institute!" cried Granny.

# CHAPTER 42
# The Lady Chairman

Mrs Wolfgruber was joined on the stage by Miss Rustling, her green dress flowing out behind her. Miss Boyle came next, yawning loudly despite all the excitement. Miss Jean followed, patting her dark hair into place and reapplying her deep red lipstick, and finally Miss Homely, who didn't seem to know where she was.

"The LPI," repeated Granny. "What are you doing here?"

"They've come to save us," shouted Dad, still pinned down by four bogles.

"Winch up the boy," growled Mrs Wolfgruber.

"And bring Daddy up here," said Miss Jean, flashing him a brilliant smile.

The bogles on top of Dad looked questioningly at Burpina, who gave them a slight nod of the head. They climbed off and pushed him roughly up on to the stage. He ran to where Mum was still slumped on the ground. Miss Jean knelt down beside him and checked Mum's head.

"She'll be all right," she said, pulling him away. "It's just a nasty bruise, but I have some wonderful cover-up make-up."

"Are you all right, Barnaby?" called Miss Rustling as he was hoisted up high.

"Yes," he yelled. "Can you get me out of this thing?"

"All in good time, darling boy," she breathed, "all in good time."

"Talking of time," said Miss Boyle, checking her watch, "let's get this thing over and done with. It's well past my nap time."

"And how exactly do you plan on helping us?" asked Granny, staring out at the army of bogles.

"Help *you*?" repeated Miss Boyle.

Granny looked at Dad.

"You said they were here to save us," she said.

"Yes," said Dad, uncertainly. "The LPI arrived back at *Ho-flay* Pickles when Morley came to get me. I knew something was wrong the minute I saw him, and they offered to help."

"Dear Mr Figg," whispered Miss Jean. "You look so handsome when you're confused. You are right, we did offer to help – but we didn't mean you."

Barnaby's heart dropped as he listened to the conversation below. Dad stared open-mouthed and Granny started glinting dangerously.

"Have you met our Lady Chairman?" continued Miss Jean. "Let me present Mrs Ball."

Burpina stepped forward, a victorious smirk on her whiskery old face.

"It's short for Ballybog," she said. "Congratulations, ladies. I was wondering how you were going to get this man here. Now I have the whole family, and Hogsflesh Pickles will be mine, all mine."

"And ours," said Miss Boyle. "We had a deal, remember?"

"Yes, yes, of course," muttered Burpina. "But that wretched whisker-fink destroyed the legal documents."

Barnaby looked over to where the extra-large bogle was holding a struggling, growling sack. Mum was still unconscious on the floor. Dad and Granny were flanked by the Ladies' Pickled Institute, and scores of bogles surrounded the stage. The situation was hopeless.

"I had my own legal documents drawn up,"

said Miss Boyle. "I wanted to make sure the LPI got a fair share of the factory."

"I'm sure you did," said Burpina. "Where are they?"

"Miss Homely," called Miss Boyle. "Did you remember to bring the papers, by any chance?"

"Dance?" asked Miss Homely, gazing out at the crowd before her. "It's been a while since I was on stage..." She started tapping her feet on the wooden platform. "... and to perform for such a large audience ... but I think I've still got a bit of the old magic."

"Stop it!" yelled Miss Boyle, as Miss Homely tap-danced across the floor. "What do you think you're doing?"

"Well, why are we on a stage in front of an audience of small beardy people, then?" she asked.

"We are here to carry out our evil plan," yelled

Miss Jean in frustration, "to destroy Beatrix *Ho-flay* and take over her factory."

"That sounds nice, dear," said Miss Homely, giving a little bow to a couple of bewildered but applauding bogles. "Do you want the papers you gave me earlier?"

Burpina rolled her eyes and snatched the documents out of Miss Homely's hands.

"Idiots!" she screamed, striding over to Granny. "Now, you sign these papers or so help me, I will turn the lot of you into chutney."

"Not so fast, darling girl," said Miss Rustling, stepping in front of her.

Burpina's mouth dropped open. She had never been called "darling girl" in her life. Mrs Wolfgruber stomped across the platform and stood beside Miss Rustling, her arms folded. Burpina took a step back, her face turning a deep, angry purple.

"What are you doing?" she roared. "Get out of my way!"

"I'm afraid that's not possible," said Miss Rustling, politely.

The rest of the LPI looked at one another in stunned silence as Burpina continued to fume.

"You see, Mrs Wolfgruber and myself," continued Miss Rustling, "are undercover agents sent by the National LPI to infiltrate this branch of bad gherkins."

There was a loud gasp as Miss Jean, Miss Boyle and Miss Homely turned white.

# CHAPTER 43
# The Battle of the LPI

"Traitors!" shouted Miss Jean.

"No, it is you who are the traitors, darling," said Miss Rustling. "You are a disgrace to the good name of the Ladies' Pickled Institute. Rumours of Mrs *Ho-flay's* dark pickles had reached LPI headquarters. But it was your unhealthy interest in them that worried everyone at HQ the most. And when Mrs Wolfgruber and I arrived, we were dismayed to find out you had already been seduced by the dark side."

"The LPI needs the dark pickles," said Miss Boyle, her baggy eyes looking more alert than

Barnaby had ever seen them. "They would make us rich and powerful."

"Look where it's led you already," said Miss Rustling, pointing towards the dangling Barnaby. "The pickling of an innocent young boy."

"You should be ashamed of yourselves," said Mrs Wolfgruber.

"I certainly would be ashamed of myself if I smelled of meatballs," said Miss Jean.

Mrs Wolfgruber started growling quietly, then launched herself at Miss Jean. "I'll give you meatballs," she yelled, pulling Miss Jean's black hair. It came completely off in her hands.

"You fiend!" cried Miss Jean. "Give me back my wig."

Mrs Wolfgruber held it high above her head. "Come and get it!" she barked.

But Miss Jean was already charging towards her. She pushed Mrs Wolfgruber off the platform into the crowd below, knocking over the bogle holding Morley in the sack. The little dog leapt out, barking loudly. The bogles nearby began screaming again as Miss Jean stage-dived off the platform, landing on top of Mrs Wolfgruber. Barnaby could just make out the old women in amongst the panicking crowd. Miss Jean had retrieved her wig and was now being chased through the terrified bogles by a furious Mrs Wolfgruber.

Miss Boyle grasped Miss Rustling's arm. "Call off that wolf woman," she screamed.

"Certainly not!" said Miss Rustling.

"Call her off!" she shrieked, shaking Miss Rustling, causing her high hair to fall down and scatter around her shoulders.

"Unhand me, you baggy-eyed buffoon," cried Miss Rustling, trying to shake Miss Boyle off. But Miss Homely grabbed hold of her other arm and the pair of them pulled Miss Rustling to the floor.

"Miss Homely," cried Miss Rustling, from beneath them both. "You are fighting for the wrong side. Your friends have turned to the dark side of pickling. Join Mrs Wolfgruber and I, and fight for onions, gherkins and chutney."

"I might be slightly hard of hearing, dear," said Miss Homely, "but I'm not stupid. I want that factory just as much as the others and I intend to get it."

Miss Rustling gasped, and grabbed them both by an ear.

"Then prepare to fail!" she shouted, rolling over on top of them.

The tangle of old women kept on rolling, right off the wooden stage, following Miss Jean and Mrs Wolfgruber, who were now wrestling below. Morley continued charging around, snapping at the heels of the scattering, screaming bogles.

Barnaby looked down at the chaos and saw his dad signalling to him that he intended to take the winch from the twitching Musty and lower him to safety. But as Dad crept up behind him, Burpina looked away from the fighting LPI straight towards him.

"Musty," she screeched, "look behind you."

The burly bogle jerked round just in time to see Dad leap on top of him.

Burpina thrust the legal papers into a bewildered Baldric's hand.

"Make her sign these," she said, running towards a grappling Dad and Musty. "It's time that boy was pickled."

Granny pulled against the tight grip Baldric was holding her in.

"I do not wish to perform a kizami tsuki on my own father," she said, "but unless you let me go right now, I'm afraid I will have to. Your great-grandson is in grave danger."

"I'm not your father, and he's not my great-grandson," said Baldric, frowning.

"Oh, wake up and smell the beetroot!" shouted Granny, impatiently. "You have been duped for years. Cheated out of your family, cheated out of your inheritance. You were the Chieftain of Bogle Bog. She's taken the leadership from you."

Barnaby could hear Granny shouting at Baldric, but he was more concerned with what was happening below him. Burpina had barged past the fighting Musty and Dad and had hold of the winch wheel. She looked up at him, a malevolent smile spreading over her horrid little face.

"Bye bye, Barnaby," she said as she lowered the dunker towards the vinegar. But just as his bottom touched the surface of the liquid, the rope jolted and began to rise again. He looked down to see Ptolemy winding as fast as he could. Dad had hold of both Musty and Burpina. Granny was still struggling with Baldric.

"It is you who should be their leader, not Burpina," she was yelling. "You are the true bogle Chieftain. You are descended from Gaseous the Great himself."

Barnaby felt the rope stop again. Burpina had broken free from Dad and was hauling Ptolemy away from the winch.

"Help me!" Ptolemy shouted down to the bogles below, still being herded like sheep by an excited Morley. "Help me save the boy."

"Shut your grub hole," screamed Burpina, grabbing the back of his smock and lifting him into the air.

"PTOLEMY!" cried Barnaby, as Burpina flung him off the platform. He landed with a thud and was quickly surrounded by a large group of bogles.

Burpina turned towards the winch, as Musty twitched right past her and off the platform again. Dad was trying to push over the giant vat. Barnaby could see it wobbling beneath him.

"Hold on, Barnaby," shouted Dad, as Burpina raced towards him. "I'm going to knock this over and—"

Barnaby watched in horror as Burpina barged into Dad, knocking him into the crowd below. She glanced up briefly at him before spinning the winch with all her might.

# CHAPTER 44
## Plummeting

For the second time in two days, Barnaby found himself plummeting to the ground. Only this time it wasn't the hard earth beneath him, but a huge vat of deadly vinegar. And once again, he felt strangely calm as time seemed to slow down. The events of a couple of seconds appeared to happen in a couple of minutes.

As his hair shot up with the force of the drop, he saw two figures emerge and grab a gloating Burpina roughly from behind. It was Granny and Baldric. And behind them came Mrs Wolfgruber and Miss Rustling, closely followed by the rest of the LPI. Everyone looked like they were moving in silent slow motion.

He could feel his feet and legs enter the cold liquid below and took a deep breath as Ptolemy, Hogarth and a large group of bogles came charging towards him. Barnaby could just make out Ptolemy's horrified face as his head went completely under.

# CHAPTER 45
## Justice for the LPI

Barnaby sat up in a pool of vinegar and smashed glass. Ptolemy was bending over him.

"He's OK," Ptolemy shouted.

Morley bounded up and licked his cheek as Mum, Dad and Granny crowded above him.

"For pickles' sake, give the boy some air," yelled Granny, pushing everyone out of the way.

Barnaby rolled on to his side and coughed up some vinegar. It burned his throat on the way up.

"I think I'm all right," he said, studying his hands and arms, which were covered in small cuts from the shattered glass vat. "What happened? Why aren't I pickled?"

Granny dipped her finger in the pool of vinegar on the floor and sniffed it contemptuously.

"Because thankfully," she said, "Burpina couldn't pickle a pepper in a preservative if her life depended on it. She should stick to toe-knuckle potion. This isn't dark pickling fluid, this is just plain malt vinegar. It's not nearly strong enough to pickle a human being. That's why your mum was OK."

Mum grinned down at him.

"I'm all right," she said, "apart from this massive bruise on my temple. It's you we're all worried about. It wouldn't have been so bad if you knew how to swim."

"You could have drowned if it wasn't for young Ptolemy here," said Granny. She patted a beaming Ptolemy on the head. "He and Hogarth led a charge of bogles straight into the vat, knocking it flying," she continued. "That's why there's glass and vinegar everywhere. He was magnificent."

Ptolemy's grin stretched through the bruises on his face.

"Thank you, Aunty Beatrix," he said.

"No – thank you, Ptolemy," she smiled.

Barnaby grinned and held his hand out to Ptolemy, who grabbed it and pulled him to his feet. He wanted to thank him, but it seemed such a small thing to say to someone who'd just saved his life. And he really wanted to say sorry for the way he had treated him.

"Hogarth helped too," said Ptolemy.

Barnaby turned to the swarthy bogle. "Thank you," he said. "I'm sorry for calling you Tufty-Nose."

"I thought it was a compliment," snorted Hogarth.

Barnaby smiled.

"You're not as scary as you look," he said.

"And your mother is a lot scarier than she looks," smiled Hogarth, bowing towards Mum. "I have learned a lot about humans today."

"You have learned nothing, you traitor," shrieked a voice from behind.

Barnaby turned to see Burpina pulling away from her brother, Baldric.

"Let go of me!" she shrieked.

"You no longer give the orders round here," said Baldric, "I do." He nodded towards the B-Team, who were being rounded up by a large band of bogles. "Your bodyguards can't help you now. You have been poisoning me for years; wiping my memory and stealing my rightful place as Chieftain of Bogle Bog. But worst of all…"

Baldric turned to Granny, holding out his long wrinkled hand to her. "You robbed me of my beautiful daughter, Beatrix."

For once in her life, Granny seemed lost for words.

Her big bottom lip trembled like a dollop of strawberry jelly, as she lifted a hand towards his.

"Rubbish!" cried Burpina, swiping Granny's hand away. She turned to address the assembled bogles. "Don't listen to him. His brain is addled; tainted by humans."

"Talking of addled brains," said a low breathy voice, "I have one right here."

Miss Rustling came barging through the crowd, bringing a dishevelled Miss Homely behind her. Mrs Wolfgruber followed with Miss

Boyle and Miss Jean. They all looked completely bedraggled, apart from Mrs Wolfgruber, whose Brillo pad hair stayed resolutely in place. Miss Jean's red lipstick was smeared down her face and her wig was on backwards, and Miss Rustling's long bushy hair was reaching out wildly in every direction.

"We intend to bring these three ladies before the national committee, for crimes against the Ladies' Pickled Institute," announced Miss Rustling. "Miss Can-Can is flying in from New Zealand to reside over the hearing personally."

"No!" cried Miss Homely, tearfully. "It's not our fault."

"She made us do it," wailed Miss Boyle, pointing at Burpina.

"She came to our meetings and told us all about the dark side of pickling, and how it would make us rich and powerful. She said that *Ho-flay* Pickles held the secret, and if we wanted to be a part of it, then we had to get as much information as possible and bring it back to her."

Barnaby pointed accusingly at Miss Homely. "That's what you were doing in the secret tunnel back at the factory," he said. "You were spying. You weren't looking for the lavatory."

"I *was* looking for a laboratory," sniffed Miss Homely, "I was spying."

"That's what I just – oh never mind," sighed Barnaby. "Did you know she was a bogle?"

"It didn't matter to us what she was," said Miss Boyle. "We just wanted that factory. She told us the dark pickles were originally her idea, but Mrs *Ho-flay* had stolen her recipes."

"Ridiculous!" fumed Granny.

"She said she had devised a plan to bring down Mrs *Ho-flay* and take over the factory," continued Miss Boyle. "But we didn't know the full details, and we certainly wouldn't have let anything happen to the boy. That was too much, even for us."

"Burpina promised to change pickling as we know it," wept Miss Jean. "That's why we made her our Lady Chairman. We did it for the LPI."

"That will be for the national committee to

decide," boomed Mrs Wolfgruber.

Miss Rustling made her way through the crowd to where Granny stood.

"Mrs *Ho-flay*," she said, sternly. "Having infiltrated this particular branch of the LPI, there is no doubt in my mind that you were producing dark pickles, which is in direct breach of the international pickling code of conduct."

Granny said nothing, but her skin began to glow.

"However," continued Miss Rustling, "Mr Figg has led us to believe that you are moving away from this vile practice, towards the special pickles, which are gaining worldwide approval."

"Barnaby is in charge of Special Pickles," said Granny, "and we are very pleased with his progress."

"Quite," said Miss Rustling, smiling at Barnaby. "He is a very special young man. With this in mind, we are willing to overlook any dark tendencies you may have, on one condition."

"Which is?" asked Granny.

Miss Rustling pointed to Burpina.

"Bogles are not widely accepted in the human world," she said. "Bringing one to justice for her crimes against the LPI would be a long and complicated business. May I trust in you to dispense the necessary punishment?"

"You may," said Granny, glowering at Burpina.

"Then we have a deal," smiled Miss Rustling. "Goodbye, Mrs *Ho-flay*, and I hope our paths cross again in happier circumstances. Goodbye, Barnaby. I'll be watching your career with interest."

"Goodbye, Miss Rustling," said Barnaby, "and thank you. Goodbye, Mrs Wolfgruber."

Barnaby and his family watched as the two old ladies dragged the other three away towards the ladder. Several small bogle children were skipping behind, flicking acorns at them. Mrs Wolfgruber spun around.

"MEATBALLS!" she roared, and they all fled in terror.

# CHAPTER 46
# The Chieftain of Bogle Bog

"What a waste of time they were," shouted Burpina as the LPI disappeared around the corner. "I should never have trusted humans – weak, cowardly creatures."

"Barnaby's not weak or cowardly," said Ptolemy.

"That's because he's only part human," said Burpina.

There was a lot of murmuring and grunting from the surrounding bogles.

"So the rumours are true," said Hogarth. "Ptolemy was right. They are related."

"Like I said before," said Burpina. "It all happened a long time ago."

"It's true," said Baldric, pointing to Granny. "This *is* my daughter. I had a human wife, long before most of you were born. She was accepted by a large part of our community, but never by my sister Burpina. She hated her."

"But she tricked you into marrying her, Baldric," cried Burpina.

"We loved each other," he said, "very much."

Burpina's frown deepened.

"And she stole my baby, Belchetta," she hissed.

"That was a mistake," said Barnaby. "She didn't mean to take your baby. She thought she was abandoned."

"Bogles never abandon their children," snapped Burpina.

"That's right," said Baldric, taking Granny's

hand, and giving it a squeeze. "Bogles never abandon their children – not even when they are nearly one hundred years old."

Barnaby thought he saw a tear well up in Granny's eye, but she blinked it away and burped loudly instead.

"Burpina poisoned my human wife with an overdose of toe-knuckle potion," continued Baldric.

There was more talking and murmuring from the crowd.

"And then," he shouted above the noise, "she fed me small doses every day. She told me it was medicine to help clear my head. But as we all know, toe-knuckle potion clouds the mind. And so eventually, the memories of my wife and daughter were erased, and Burpina took my place as Chieftain of Bogle Bog, saying I was unfit to rule. She forbade any mention of my human wife and slowly, over many years, it turned into a rumour."

"That was until I arrived," said Ptolemy to Barnaby's mum and dad. "My great-grandmother was Uncle Baldric and Aunt Burpina's little sister – Windianna Ballybog. She married Tuber Tatty and went off to live with the Tatty bogles. But she remembered all about what they called *the human connection*. When I came to live in Bogle Bog, I was very curious about my human cousin, Barnaby, and went off to find him."

"You interfering little twerp," fumed Burpina. "You have ruined everything."

"It's not Ptolemy's fault. You kidnapped my daughter," said Granny.

"You pickled *my* daughter," shouted Burpina.

"She tried to murder us," cried Barnaby.

"She was just trying to get what was rightfully ours," said Burpina. "Hogsflesh Pickles."

"*Ho-flay*," corrected Granny, "and I think you have proved, with this pickling debacle —" she pointed to the smashed vinegar vats —"that you have no idea how to pickle things correctly. So I obviously didn't steal any of your recipes."

"I might not have got the ingredients exactly right this time," said Burpina, "but I will. Because my potions inspired you and led you to the dark side."

"I've turned my back on that sort of thing," said Granny, haughtily.

"Well, I haven't," muttered Burpina, "and if it wasn't for me, you wouldn't even have a factory. And one day, Beatrix Hogsflesh," she said, deliberately pronouncing it incorrectly, much to Granny's annoyance, "I intend to have it."

Granny's face turned puce. She looked like she was about to pounce on Burpina, but Baldric took a step between them, and turned to address the assembled bogles again.

"I think we have heard enough," he said. "Burpina, do you admit to feeding me toe-knuckle potion every day for over fifty years?"

"I did it for you, you idiot," she screeched. "You were tricked into that marriage."

"I was happy in that marriage," Baldric said. "And do you admit to the unlawful takeover of the bogle chieftainship?"

"I had no choice," she said. "You were in no position to do it, and I was next in line."

"Actually, my daughter is next in line," said Baldric.

Granny's eyes widened in horror at the thought of living in the bog and ruling the bogles.

"Impossible!" screamed Burpina. "Only those of pure bogle blood can rule us."

"Thank goodness for that," Granny whispered in Barnaby's ear.

Baldric frowned, but continued his speech. "And do you admit to the kidnapping of this woman," he said, pointing at Mum, "who also happens to be my granddaughter? And the attempted pickling of my great-grandson, Barnaby?"

"They deserved it," snarled Burpina.

"Then, by the authority vested in me as Chieftain of Bogle Bog," said Baldric in a loud clear voice, "I hereby banish you from this place for ever, under penalty of memory loss by toe-knuckle potion."

# CHAPTER 47
# A National Bogle Holiday

A long procession of bogles led Burpina out of the Landing Square and through the narrow streets to the long ladder that led up to the hollow tree. Baldric, Ptolemy and Hogarth were at the head, Burpina and the B-Team in the middle, and Barnaby holding Morley tightly on a lead, with Granny, Mum and Dad at the back.

"You can't banish me," Burpina was screaming. "I am your leader."

"You're not our leader," shouted one of the crowd.

"Baldric is the true leader," said Hogarth.

They approached the bottom of the ladder. The B-Team slowly began the long climb, one by one. Musty was first. The pickled worm burps had nearly worn off, and he had almost stopped twitching, a slight jerk of the head the only sign he had been exposed to them.

"Traitors," he shouted. "Burpina is the true Bogle Chieftain now. Baldric lost his right to rule the minute he married a human."

"Get moving," yelled Baldric, poking Musty's bottom with his walking stick.

Musty shot up the ladder, quickly followed by the rest. Burpina climbed a short way and then turned to face the crowd.

"You have let these humans corrupt your minds," she yelled. "Human beings are our sworn enemies."

"We like annoying them," cried a short, plump bogle. His spiky beard almost touched the ground, and Barnaby thought he looked like an enormous hedgehog. "But we don't want to kidnap them."

"Or pickle them," shouted another.

"Then you are fools," she shouted. "This is your last chance to join me or stay here and rot."

There was complete silence. Nobody moved.

"So be it," she said, turning to Granny. Her black eyes seemed to be glowing red with fury. "But I still want my revenge."

"A beard for a beard would make the whole world bald," said Granny. "Is that what you want?"

"You know what I want," hissed Burpina, as she began the long climb. "Always keep looking over your shoulder, Beatrix Hogsflesh."

"I won't need to," Granny called up. "I would smell you the minute you came within half a mile. Now, be off with you."

Everyone started talking at once as Burpina disappeared up the ladder and through the hollow tree. Ptolemy pushed through the crowd and stood next to Barnaby.

"Do you think she'll come back?" asked Barnaby.

"I doubt it," said Ptolemy. "She won't want a dose of her own medicine; although she could do with it."

"I wonder where she will go," said Barnaby.

"To the Shellycoats, I expect."

"Where's that?"

"Not where, but who," answered Ptolemy. "The Shellycoats are another clan of bogles. Not as hairy as the Ballybogs or as fierce as the Tattys. She was married to one a very long time ago – Grimly Shellycoat."

"I didn't know she was married," said Barnaby.

"Yes, he was Belchetta's father. Apparently, Burpina went to Shellycoat Marsh with Grimly and returned to Bogle Bog one year later with her baby, Belchetta. Burpina said that Grimly had died of marsh fever and she wanted to stay here and remain a Ballybog."

"How do you know all this?" asked Barnaby.

"My great-granny told me – Windianna. She was Baldric and Burpina's little sister – remember?"

"Is she still alive?"

"No, she died a while ago," said Ptolemy, sadly. "But it's because of her that I found you."

"Well then, I'm very grateful to Windianna too," said Barnaby, "because if it wasn't for her, then I would never have found my little bogle cousin."

Ptolemy's face glowed pink with pleasure as Baldric turned to face the noisy crowd. He held his hands up for quiet.

"Fellow bogles," he shouted. "For the past fifty years, my brain has been clouded with poison. I haven't been able to think for myself, and my sister has ruled over you with fear and hatred. It's time for change."

A big cheer went up.

"Yes, we have fierce tempers, and we love to annoy humans, but no more kidnappings or picklings. I promise you a return to our old bogling ways – making humans hear voices round corners when no one is there –"

There was a lot of laughter.

"– entering houses and making a mess –"

More whooping.

"– and causing things to happen at the wrong time."

Mum and Dad looked slightly uncomfortable and Barnaby glanced nervously at Granny as the gathered bogles shouted and clapped their appreciation.

"They can't stop being bogles," whispered

Granny, "and causing mischief is better than kidnapping people and pickling them."

Barnaby shrugged his shoulders.

"I suppose so," he said. He was slowly getting used to his strange relations.

"I might be nearly one hundred years old," shouted Baldric, "but there's life in the old bogle yet."

The crowd went mad and hoisted him up on their shoulders. They surged back towards the Landing Square, Ptolemy at the front, chanting,

"BALDRIC, BALDRIC, BALDRIC."

Baldric sailed high above them, waving his walking stick in the air, enjoying himself immensely.

"Light the fires," he bellowed, "call the musicians. I hereby proclaim today as a national bogle holiday!"

Barnaby, Granny, Mum and Dad stood at the bottom of the ladder and watched the jubilant procession of bogles go. Morley tugged on his lead, barking at them.

"They seem to have forgotten about us," said Dad, slightly relieved.

"I don't think they would notice if we nipped up the ladder and went home," said Mum.

Barnaby didn't want to go. He had seen a different side to the bogles, and he still hadn't said thank you to Ptolemy for saving his life. He looked at Granny, who was watching the last bogle disappear around the corner. She kept looking a long time after he had gone.

"I suppose there's no point staying here," she sighed.

"Do you want to go after them, Granny?" asked Barnaby. "After all, you have just discovered your long-lost dad."

"I don't think so," she said, looking up the big ladder. "Onwards and upwards, Barnaby.

We don't belong here. Let's just hope I don't get stuck again."

"I've just realized," he said, "you haven't sneezed for ages. I think your cold must have cleared up."

"I think it was the shock of seeing you plunging into that vinegar," said Granny.

She had just put her foot on the first rung when Ptolemy came tearing round the corner.

"Where are you going?" he shouted.

"Home," said Barnaby.

"You can't go home – you'll miss the party and you're our guests of honour," said Ptolemy.

"But we're humans," said Dad. "I mean, I am and they are … sort of."

"Exactly," grinned Ptolemy, grabbing Barnaby by the hand and dragging him along. "Have you ever been to a bogle bop?"

"Never," laughed Barnaby.

"Then you're in for a treat. Come on."

# CHAPTER 48
## Brogles

When they arrived back in the square, a huge bonfire was being lit in the centre. The wooden stage was cleared of the broken glass vats and a small group of bogles trooped up the steps. The largest one was rolling a hollow tree stump. He stopped in the centre of the stage and heaved it over. Barnaby could see that an animal skin had been stretched across the top. The big bogle began beating it with two massive sticks.

"It's a drum," cried Barnaby in delight.

"That's right," said Ptolemy, wiggling his hips

to the beat. "Wait till you hear the bladder-pipes."

A low droning sound filled the air, mixing hauntingly with the drums. Barnaby watched in wonder as a small bogle with the most enormous hands pumped a round bag. Two more bogles stood either side of him, each holding a long pipe attached to the bag. The second their long bony fingers moved up and down the pipes, the most curious melody burst out. A big cheer went up and all the bogles began a strange dance around the huge fire. Mum and Dad looked on in astonishment as Baldric pulled Granny into the jumping crowd and began twirling her around the floor.

"Come on, Beatrix," he shouted. "We've got fifty years of bogle bops to catch up on."

"I'm a bit out of practice," she laughed, jerking her knees in time to the drum.

"They look like they've had a dose of worm

burps," chuckled Barnaby.

"Who would have thought that a pig's bladder could make such a fantastic sound?" yelled Ptolemy, whose legs were moving so fast, Barnaby could hardly see them.

"Humans have something similar," shouted Barnaby, above the music. "They're called bagpipes, but it only takes one person to play them, not three."

"The more the merrier, I say," puffed Ptolemy. "Listen, here comes the xylobone."

Barnaby looked up at the stage. The drummer and pipers were joined by two more musicians. One was striking a long line of different-length bones with a small hammer, the other strumming frenziedly on a small guitar.

"Is that a guitar?" asked Barnaby, slightly relieved to see something familiar.

"Kind of," said Ptolemy. "The strings are

made of strengthened mucous membranes. It's called a catarrh. And here's the harp player."

Barnaby wrinkled his nose. "Are the harp strings made of mucus too?"

"Don't be silly," said Ptolemy, "it's just a normal harp."

"Thank goodness for that."

"A normal worm harp," continued Ptolemy. "The worms are stretched to different lengths to create a range of notes. Now, enough talking, let's dance."

Barnaby tied an exhausted Morley to a tree, and he promptly flopped down and closed his eyes, despite all the noise and excitement around him. Ptolemy pulled Barnaby into the circle of dancing bogles. Granny and Baldric twirled by.

"I'll show you how to dance like a bogle," said Ptolemy. "You have to keep your top half completely still, except for your arms, which have to strike a pose." He bent his wrists and elbows at different angles, making him look like an ancient Egyptian dancer. Barnaby followed. "Then you have to jig your feet." Ptolemy's legs started moving ten to the dozen. Barnaby tried to keep up. "Faster," shouted Ptolemy. "Get those knees higher. Now, strike a new pose with your top half." He flicked his arms round to frame his hairy face. "But keep your legs going, don't stop – that's it, you're doing it. But don't smile – surly and silent, even when you're enjoying yourself."

Barnaby whirled and twirled around the fire with Ptolemy, trying his hardest not to laugh. Eventually they

collided and landed in a heap on the floor.

"Let's rest for a while," panted Barnaby. "I'm exhausted."

"Me too," wheezed a bright red Ptolemy.

They moved a little way away from the partying bogles and sat on a large rock watching the festivities.

"I need to thank you for saving me," said Barnaby.

Ptolemy grinned and shuffled up closer to him. "That's what cousins are for," he said.

"I think that makes us more than just cousins," Barnaby continued. "You saved my life. You're more a—"

"What?" asked Ptolemy, eagerly.

"Brother. Bogle brothers or brother bogles."

"Brogles!" cried Ptolemy, his spiky face lighting up in the gloom. They sat next to each other, knees touching, in companionable silence, watching the party.

Barnaby could see his parents joining in with the dancing. Mum's laughing face was lit up by the enormous bonfire. Granny had attracted her own little circle of bogles and appeared to be showing them some break-dance moves. Ptolemy looked questioningly at Barnaby.

"She can do anything and everything," laughed Barnaby.

As he watched his family dancing with the bogles, Barnaby knew that he would never have any more bogle nightmares. He smiled and put his arm around Ptolemy. He was finally coming to terms with his bogleness, and suddenly realized what that tiny fraction of bogle inside him had been waiting for. This very moment.

The End .